Eden's
EVERDARK

ALSO BY KAREN STRONG

Just South of Home

Eden's
EVERDARK

KAREN STRONG

Simon & Schuster Books for Young Readers

NEW YORK LONDON TORONTO SYDNEY NEW DELHI

SIMON & SCHUSTER BOOKS FOR YOUNG READERS

An imprint of Simon & Schuster Children's Publishing Division

1230 Avenue of the Americas, New York, New York 10020

SIMON & SCHUSTER BOOKS FOR YOUNG READERS

and related marks are trademarks of Simon & Schuster, Inc.

For information about special discounts for bulk purchases, please contact Simon & Schuster Special Sales at 1-866-506-1949 or business@simonandschuster.com.

The Simon & Schuster Speakers Bureau can bring authors to your live event. For more information or to book an event, contact the Simon & Schuster Speakers Bureau at 1-866-248-3049 or visit our website at www.simonspeakers.com.

Interior design by Hilary Zarycky

The text for this book was set in Adobe Jenson Pro.

Manufactured in the United States of America

0722 FFG

First Edition

2 4 6 8 10 9 7 5 3 1

Library of Congress Cataloging-in-Publication Data

Names: Strong, Karen, author.

Title: Eden's Everdark / Karen Strong.

Description: First edition. | New York : Simon & Schuster Books for Young Readers, 2022. | Audience: Ages 8–12. | Audience: Grades 4–6. | Summary: Twelve-year-old Eden, on a visit to her late mother's birthplace of Safina Island, Georgia, discovers a creepy sketchbook that leads her to Everdark—a spirit world ruled by an evil witch who Eden must defeat in order to make it back home.

Identifiers: LCCN 2021047148 | ISBN 9781665904476 (hardcover) | ISBN 9781665904490 (ebook)

Subjects: CYAC: Magic—Fiction. | Witches—Fiction. | Fantasy. | LCGFT: Fantasy fiction.

Classification: LCC PZ7.1.S79642 Ed 2022 | DDC [Fic]—dc23

LC record available at https://lccn.loc.gov/2021047148

For all who know grief.
In the deepest darkness, hope can still bloom.

Eden's
EVERDARK

CHAPTER ONE

Glass Flower

Eden slid her finger on the map to the blue expanse of the Atlantic Ocean. She stared at the sea islands off the coast of Georgia. The largest island was out farther than the rest, an isolated mass. This was Safina Island, her mother's birthplace.

Her father had bought the map at a North Carolina rest stop and designated her as the navigator instead of using the app on his phone. It was an opportunity for Eden to learn the geography of intersecting routes and identify points of interest.

On their road trip, they ate junk food from vending machines and drank too much soda. They sang songs and laughed at their off-key melodies. It could have been easy to pretend that it had always been just the two of them, but a weight pressed heavy on Eden's chest like a block of ice. The cold truth of her mother's death.

She had endured the first days of shock with denial. Then a bitter acceptance when the house stopped being full of strangers offering their condolences with dishes wrapped in foil. During this time her father had treated Eden like a glass flower, a fragile girl who could break at the slightest touch. But when the record heat of the summer turned into the chill of winter snow, Eden's father slowly transferred his energy back into his work. A professor of evolutionary biology, he was teaching a full course load for the semester. Dr. Langston Leopold was keeping himself very busy.

Today he was dressed similarly to Eden in a graphic tee and jeans—much different from his usual uniform of oxford shirt and khaki pants. But he still wore his tortoiseshell glasses that complemented his brown skin.

"Saw a sign for a diner a few miles back," he said. "Should be coming up soon."

They were traveling the local highway through the coastal town of Marien, Georgia. The trees were different from the ones in Maryland. The pines had skinny trunks, and wide oaks dripped with Spanish moss. Palmettos clustered together as if sharing secrets. Eden hadn't seen any of the red clay that she had read about online. Instead the soil was sandy brown as if the beach had invaded the mainland.

"Do you think this place will have fried green tomatoes?" Eden asked.

"I'll bet they do." Dr. Leopold chuckled, but then his face turned solemn. "You still feeling okay about this trip? It's not too much, is it?"

A knot formed in Eden's stomach. Those words again: *too much.*

They had lost the same person and been through the same journey together. Couldn't he understand this was her chance to meet her mother's family? Eden couldn't explain how a place she had never visited could feel so much like home. How could she describe that kind of yearning to her father? Nothing could ever be too much for Eden. Not even the universe could fill the empty space her mother had left.

"Remember, you have to tell me." Dr. Leopold stumbled in her silence. "If you're not okay, you have to let me know."

He was treating Eden like a glass flower again, so different from her mother, who always trusted that she had the strength to handle things. To bend but not break to whatever the world gave her. Strong enough not to shatter into tiny shards.

"Dad, this is my family," Eden finally said. "This is my chance to finally meet them."

Dr. Leopold ran his hand over his cropped curls, a nervous tic. "I just don't want this visit to make you sad."

"I'm already sad," Eden answered.

"I know," her father stated quietly.

They were still in grief counseling. It had been good for both of them, although difficult. Eden had spent the first session watching her father weep. It was in a recent session that the decision had been made to visit Safina Island as a healing balm. Dr. Leopold was reluctant about the idea at first, but when Eden persisted, he finally agreed.

Her mother's childhood on the island was murky. Eden knew Safina Island was where her enslaved ancestors had cultivated cotton and sugar cane. It was these ancestors who'd stayed on the island during the Civil War when their enslavers had fled. When the federal government had granted them land after the war, they made the island their home. When the former enslavers returned, the federal government stripped the free people of their granted land. But her mother's family had been able to purchase the entire north side of Safina Island.

The Gardener family had stayed. They'd stayed through

famine and hurricanes. They'd stayed through failed attempts of golf courses and luxury hotels. The Gardener family persevered and had lived on their land for over two centuries.

Every spring her mother's family held a celebration on Safina Island. Eden knew about these anniversaries of the Gardener land purchase from the invitations in pale blue envelopes sent by her great-aunt. The same one who also sent Eden birthday cards every year with a pressed island flower and a crisp twenty-dollar bill. Her mother had never wanted to attend these celebrations, so Eden had never been given a chance to visit Safina Island.

Now she was going to meet her mother's family and learn all the things that were blurred in her history.

Her mother had been twelve years old when she left the island of her ancestors. The same age Eden was now. More than anything, she wanted to know why her mother never wanted to return to her birthplace.

Elvira's Diner was tucked off a dusty side road. A few cars were parked in the small lot. Most of them had Georgia plates with faded peach decals. Eden decided this was a place to eat for the coastal town's locals.

When they entered the diner, the mostly brown faces of the patrons turned to gawk at them, but after a few awkward seconds, they returned to their conversations and food.

An older light-skinned woman in a pink apron greeted them. "Y'all want a table?"

"That would be great," Eden's father said.

The waitress scanned the parking lot. "It's just y'all two?"

Dr. Leopold put his arm around Eden's shoulder like a protective shield. "Yes, it's just me and my daughter."

The waitress led them to a leather booth with deeply cracked seats sealed with red masking tape. Eden slid in and quickly grabbed a menu.

"I'm going to find the restroom. Be back," her father said.

Eden waited until he was gone before she opened her macramé bag. She pulled out her phone and called her best friend. Natalie answered immediately.

"Are you there yet?" she asked.

"Almost. We're at a diner now. I don't think it's far from the dock."

"Is your dad still acting weird?" Natalie asked.

"Yep," Eden answered.

Hearing Natalie's voice instantly calmed her. Natalie had been Eden's best friend since her first day at Cathedral, the Maryland private school they both attended. They quickly became chosen sisters. The Chen household was a second home to Eden. At Lunar New Year, she got her own red envelope. She would help Natalie's father put decadent fillings of minced pork and chives into dumplings, then watch him fry them to perfection. Eden would sit on Natalie's thick rug and eat them until her stomach stretched tight in her clothes.

In the days after her mother's death, Natalie had wrapped Eden in a quilt to keep the wolves of grief away. Her best friend's family had been among the small number of people who wore white in the sea of black at the memorial service.

Now Eden envisioned Natalie in her bedroom, sitting on

her thick rug wrapped in a plush terry-cloth robe with her pet rabbit, Fiver, on her lap. Surrounded by macramé cords and wooden beads for her latest craft project, she would have a cup of tea within reach for inspiration.

"I have to admit, I'm surprised your dad didn't turn around and drive you straight back to Maryland. This is true progress," Natalie said.

"It's too late for that now," Eden replied. "My uncle is coming to pick us up."

Since Safina Island had no bridges connecting it to the mainland, they would have to cross the water in her great-uncle's boat.

"Spring break will be so boring without you." Natalie paused. "Are you nervous? You'll be meeting so many people at once."

Eden was worried about this. Not only was she going to her mother's island for the first time, but she would also be meeting that entire side of her family. She hoped that she wouldn't disappoint them.

"Aunt Susanna has always wanted us to come visit. It'll be okay."

"That's true," Natalie agreed. "But I'm going to miss you! I hope I don't get so bored I decide to cut my own bangs. You won't even be here to stop me."

"Stop being so dramatic." Eden laughed. "I'll only be gone for a few days. You won't even get a chance to miss me."

Natalie was quiet for several moments, but she spoke again before Eden thought they had been disconnected.

"You've always wanted to go to Safina Island," she said softly. "I'm so happy for you."

After Eden said goodbye to her best friend, she pulled out a photograph. Last night while packing for her trip, she had taken it out of the frame she kept on her nightstand. It was the same photograph she had chosen for the memorial service program.

Her mother had been in the summer garden drenched in sunshine. They had just returned from Thyme After Thyme Nursery with packets of seeds. Eden stared at the smudges of dirt on her mother's collarbone and cheek. This was how she wanted to remember her. She turned it over and stared at the two words in her father's handwriting: *Beloved Nora.*

Dr. Nora Gardener, the botanist and professor. The woman who kept her family name when she married. The mother who filled up Eden's bedroom with glass globes full of soil and succulents.

A prick of pain twisted in Eden's eyes. Blinking back tears, she pushed the icy sadness away. This was the thing she had learned about grief. It gave no warning. She was never prepared for its sharp sting.

"Eden?" Her father's voice brought her back to the realm of the diner.

Dr. Leopold was standing beside her, his face full of concern. He stared at the photograph in her hands.

"Your mother was very happy that day," he said quietly.

Eden sniffed and put the photograph back in her purse as her father slid back into the booth and picked up the diner menu.

"Looks like they don't have fried green tomatoes," her father said, a slight disappointment in his voice.

Eden peered out the diner window. This was the closest she

had ever been to her mother's birthplace. Soon she would be on Safina Island, and questions bubbled up her throat.

"Dad?"

Her father lowered his menu. "Are you okay?"

"Why did Mom never want to come back here?"

Her father hesitated. "It's complicated."

Eden swallowed. "Are . . . are the Gardeners bad people?"

"No, of course not. They're good, hardworking people, and your mother loved her family. It was hard after the divorce when her father, your grandfather, left the island." Dr. Leopold ran a hand over his cropped curls. "Then she was in an accident and had to go to the mainland to recover. I think she never came back because all those memories haunted her."

"She never talked to me about it," Eden said. "Do you know what kind of accident—"

They were interrupted by the waitress arriving at their table with two glasses of sweet tea. "These drinks on the house. Y'all done figured out what to eat yet?"

Dr. Leopold ordered the special, and Eden ordered a cheeseburger and fries. Her father avoided meeting Eden's eyes, and she knew that he wouldn't talk any more about her mother in this public place. For now, her questions would have to remain unanswered until she arrived on the island.

CHAPTER TWO

Willow Hammock

They left the diner and drove down a dusty road to the marina. After Dr. Leopold paid for parking, they waited on the dock for her great-uncle's boat. Eden already knew that her relatives owned a touring business. They would ferry visitors from the mainland, and then take them to places of interest on the island, sharing its history.

On the north side, where most of the Gardener land was located, Willow Hammock was a small, self-sustaining village, as it had been after the Civil War. The island families had kept it going ever since.

Aunt Susanna had built several houses that rested on high stilts near the marsh. She called them birdhouse cottages, and she rented them to tourists who wanted to stay overnight on the island. Most of Willow Hammock had electricity and landlines, but there was still no cell service.

On the south side, there was a small country store, a library, and even a post office. The state university also had a marine biology research center. Other parts of the island had been designated as a nature preserve, but there was still private land owned by the former enslavers' descendants. Like the Gardener family, these ancestors also held a legacy on Safina Island.

Dr. Leopold checked his watch. "The boat should be here soon."

Eden sat on a bench and watched herons, with their long necks, dip into the water. The setting sun painted the sky a vibrant orange. Small white buildings dotted the flat land in the distance. The water was calm, and the nearby marshland filled the air with the faint scent of sulfur.

Several elderly white men laughed as they climbed up the dock, one of them pulling gear from a boat while the others grabbed large coolers. Eden assumed that they had just come in from a day of fishing. Other than the men, the dock was empty except for the tiny office where a teen boy read a hunting magazine.

A sky-blue boat settled into the harbor with a buzzy rattle, the name *Safina Queen* written in bold cursive on its side. A tall, dark-skinned man wearing shorts and a T-shirt stepped off the boat and approached them, boasting a wide smile.

"William Hall, Susanna's husband. But y'all can call me Uncle Willie. Pleasure all mine." He paused to look at Eden, inspecting her from head to toe. "Is this Little Eden? You look just like your mama. She spit you right on out."

Eden shifted closer to her father and remained quiet. Dr. Leopold shook Uncle Willie's hand. "Nice to meet you. I'm Langston. I was Nora's husband."

Eden twitched at her father's words. She hated when he spoke in the past tense about her mother. Should she introduce herself the same way? She formed the words in her head: *I was Nora's daughter.* Even unspoken, they felt tainted and wrong in her mouth.

"Eden is shy around strangers," Dr. Leopold continued. "She'll be better once we get to the island and meet everyone."

"Ain't no strangers around here," Uncle Willie said. "We all family."

Eden cracked a small smile at the tall man. His voice had a melody to its tone. Not quite Southern, at least not how she had heard it. Her great-uncle's spoken words had the origin of sun and sea.

"This the last pickup for the day," Uncle Willie said. "More coming in the morning. Let's head out. Lots of things still to do."

They gathered their luggage and followed Uncle Willie to the boat. When he cranked up the engine, the *Safina Queen* jerked alive and drifted into the open water. Eden sat starboard, the water churning in a frothy wake behind them.

"Y'all settle in and enjoy the beauty," Uncle Willie told them.

Eden breathed deeply, letting the salt tinge her tongue. Soon she would be able to sink her feet into Safina Island's soil for the very first time.

The sun was setting when they arrived, but Eden could still see Safina Island's beauty. The flatness of the marsh, pristine and untouched. Thick woodlands lush with trees and flora. A serene place where nature still dwelled and dominated.

The *Safina Queen* idled next to a newly built dock that stood on thick stilts. A narrow boardwalk led to the shore.

"Can't see much now, but at dayclean, y'all have a feast for your eyes," Uncle Willie said.

"What's 'dayclean'?" Eden asked.

"A fresh day. When light banish the dark."

After securing the boat, they retrieved their luggage and walked to a red pickup truck. Eden sat between her father and her great-uncle. The dirt road was lined with trees on both sides. Thick with Spanish moss, the live oaks seemed ancient, as if they could share the secrets of how the world was made.

Eden was quiet during the trip, craning her neck around her father to absorb the island's beauty. When they arrived at Willow Hammock, houses painted bright colors appeared along the road. In the distance, a church's steeple peeked out from the tree line, stark white in the approaching dusk.

Uncle Willie parked his truck in the yard of a mint-green house framed by fencing, where goats and chickens scurried from the noise of the engine. Aunt Susanna opened the door of the screened porch wearing a faded floral dress, a wet towel on her shoulder.

"You made it safe and sound. What a day, what a day. This baby done made it to Safina. Such a blessing." She hugged both Eden and her father.

"This place is just as beautiful as I knew it would be," Dr. Leopold said.

"Well, I should hope so," Aunt Susanna chuckled. "Come follow me. I decided y'all needed to stay with us. Birdhouses full of folks, but we got plenty of room here."

The front yard was smooth pounded dirt, as if no grass had grown there for many years, if ever. On the way to the screened porch, Eden passed a tree full of glass bottles. When she touched them, they clinked like wind chimes.

Inside the house, Aunt Susanna guided them to the kitchen, where two older women sat at a table chattering in Uncle Willie's same musical tone.

"They made it," Aunt Susanna said to the women. "My lovely niece and her daddy. This Nora's child."

The women looked at one another and spoke again between themselves, but Eden didn't understand what they said. Instead she smiled and let each of them hug her.

"I'm Mrs. Betsy Gardener," one of them said. "This my sister, Mrs. Melba Gardener. But we both Browns."

"Y'all stop confusing the girl." Aunt Susanna turned to Eden. "They trying to tell you they from the Brown family. Island born and raised. Little Betsy married Leroy, and Miss Melba married Denero."

"Still wondering if I made the right choice," Miss Melba said, laughing.

"Are you hungry, child?" Aunt Susanna asked. "I can fix you and your daddy a plate."

"No, we already ate at Elvira's Diner."

Little Betsy huffed. "My condolences."

Uncle Willie guided Eden and her father into the den, where two men lounged together on a couch watching TV.

"They made it in. Little Eden and her daddy, Dr. Langston Leopold," he announced proudly.

The elder men introduced themselves as the husbands of Little Betsy and Miss Melba, and Eden learned that her Gardener cousins lived just down the road.

Dr. Leopold went to each of the men and shook their hands.

"I understand both of you are lifelong residents of Willow Hammock."

"Ain't dead yet," Little Betsy's husband said. "We still here."

Uncle Willie chuckled. "Ain't like it used to be though. Our young-uns tend to leave and don't come back much."

"Tomorrow, they all be here," Miss Melba's husband stated. "Celebrating this land which is ours."

"Amen to that," Uncle Willie said.

Miss Melba rushed into the room. "Did I just hear Willie call you a doctor?" she asked Eden's father.

"Well, not that kind of—"

"I've been meaning to go to the mainland to see about myself. But maybe you can help, since you here. Need to talk to you about this crick in my neck."

"Leave him be," Miss Melba's husband interrupted her. "This man done crossed the water after a long journey."

"I'm not a physician, but I could still take a look at your neck," Eden's father offered.

Miss Melba furrowed her brow in confusion. "What kind of doctor are you, then?"

"I have a PhD in biology," he answered. "I teach up in Maryland."

"Ah, so you know all about them amoebas, then." Little Betsy's husband straightened up on the couch. "Do y'all remember that time when we was in school cutting open frogs and Willie passed out? Scalpel ain't even touch that frog's skin, and there he was straight out on the floor."

A rumble of laughter caught in Eden's throat, but she kept it in. She loved her family already.

"It was that awful smell. Too strong for me," Uncle Willie protested.

"Oh, I remember," Miss Melba chimed in. "Willie's knobby knees was shaking. Gut fish all his life and he was scared of the *inside* of a frog."

Uncle Willie laughed and the others joined him. Aunt Susanna arrived to investigate the commotion.

"What on earth are y'all talking about in here?" she asked.

Miss Melba turned to her. "Did you know Little Eden's daddy ain't a real doctor? He just one of them learned ones."

After Miss Melba and Little Betsy said their goodbyes, they left with their husbands. Aunt Susanna led Eden down a hallway to a room with a small bed and dark wood paneling.

"This where you gon' stay." Aunt Susanna paused. "Used to be your mama and granny's room before they left for the mainland. Now one of my guest rooms."

Eden sat on the firm bed, which faced a window to the backyard and the darkness of the woods. Her mother and grandmother had lived in this house. Slept in this very room. She moved her hands over a faded quilt.

Eden's grandmother had always been eccentric, and Eden remembered Granny Alma's island stories of laying tricks and the secret language of flowers. She had told Eden that it was an extra blessing to be born a Gardener. But the blessed lineage couldn't stop Granny Alma from turning ill. It was at her grandmother's funeral two years ago that Eden had met Aunt Susanna for the first time. Eden remembered her mother's sadness when Granny Alma passed. Back then she couldn't fully grasp the grief, but now she understood. Losing a mother was a loss that filled up the lungs with broken glass, every breath a sharp pain.

Her great-aunt sat beside her. "I miss my sister something awful, so I know how much you must miss your mama. They were taken from us too soon. May they rest in peace."

The block of ice pressed heavy on Eden's chest. Safina Island was supposed to be a healing balm, but right now all Eden felt was raw sorrow.

"I know my mom never came to these celebrations." Eden blinked away tears. "So it's an honor to be here. Thank you for inviting me."

"No need to thank me, child. Just happy you here to see Safina for yourself."

"Me too," Eden said.

Her great-aunt touched her cheek and smiled. "When the sun rise tomorrow, all will be well."

CHAPTER THREE
The Sketchbook

Eden unpacked her clothes, putting them in a small chest of drawers. On the nightstand, she propped her mother's photograph against the ceramic pot of an aloe vera plant. Touching its fleshy leaves and tiny spikes, she thought of the succulents in her bedroom back in Maryland.

She peered into a tiny closet, which was filled with extra pillows, dusty quilts, and several old boxes. The strong smell of moth balls filled up her nose, and she let out a tiny sneeze.

Eden wondered if there was a chance that some of her mother's things were in any of these boxes, abandoned and then forgotten when she left for the mainland so many years ago.

Stretching up on her tiptoes, she reached for the boxes on the closet shelf and cradled them in her arms. Eden sat cross-legged on the warm wood floor. She shuffled through the first box and found old photographs and papers. Eden stared at sepia images of family she hadn't known but recognized. The Gardener genes were strong. Dark brown skin. Eyes that tilted up at the corners. Full lips and sharp cheekbones. Eden shared all these traits with the women and men in these photographs. She closely examined each of them, but there were none of her mother.

The last box she opened was full of sketchbooks, and Eden

instantly recognized her mother's style. This was what she had hoped to find. Eden's mother had published two books of botanical art, and Eden used to accompany her to bookstores all over Maryland where she would sign copies for patrons.

These sketchbooks belonged to a girl who was still burgeoning in her craft, which only made Eden love them more because the drawings weren't polished and perfect.

She opened sketchbook after sketchbook and admired the art inside. Her mother had drawn island flowers, indigenous plants, and various herbs. She found sketchbooks with meadows filled with sweetgrass and everlasting blooms. Beaches with sea oats and pennywort. Salt marshes dense with cordgrass. But there were also drawings of ghost crabs, ibis birds, and sea turtles. Her mother's love of all living things was evident in these sketchbooks.

Eden finally came upon the last sketchbook at the bottom of the box. It was smaller than the others, bent and warped, with a sandblasted cover. The pages revealed charcoal drawings of bleak beaches, stormy oceans, and night skies. Old, wrinkled hands reaching out from a dark hallway. A mansion covered in roots and leaves. Nightscapes of live oaks, dripping in Spanish moss. Eden stared at a sketch of a black cat lurking on a seashell path. She turned the page to find a large bird with sharp claws in the silhouette of a full moon. The next page had a monstrous dog with an open mouth that revealed dagger-sharp teeth. These drawings filled Eden with a morbid familiarity, as if her mother had drawn a dark mirror of Safina Island.

Eden continued to explore the pages. There were watercolor sketches of children with dark skin—not brown like her own, but deep indigo and flecked with tiny silver stars. Girls in high-necked dresses with long pearl necklaces. Bare-chested boys who held fishing nets full of intricate knots and loops. They all had wide, bright eyes, but their mouths were frozen in eternal screams.

The last pages of the sketchbook contained drawings of a beautiful woman. Like the children, she had shimmering indigo skin and bright eyes. Her hair was windblown, a dark cotton cloud against her white flowing dress. Her long, sharp nails were painted black. At the bottom of the last sketch were tiny, blocked words: *The Witch of Everdark.*

Eden put all the sketchbooks back in the box except the one full of creepy landscapes, cursed children, and drawings of the beautiful witch. Knitting her brows, Eden wasn't sure why she felt compelled to keep it. The sketchbook had shown that her mother had an affinity for darkness, a stark contrast to the bright botanical style that Eden had always known. At times, Eden's grief felt like a shroud of eternal night, just like the world her mother had created in those pages. Maybe the drawings had spoken to the deepest part of her despair. Eden realized she was attracted to this darkness too.

The sketchbook was now also another mystery. Why had her mother drawn such morbid images? Eden felt a tug that wanted to reveal more truth. A faint recognition hummed inside her.

She placed the sketchbook on the nightstand next to her mother's photograph, and she opened the curtains to stare out the window. The woods were murky, and the full moon splashed shadows among the trees.

Eden had never dreaded the dark. At bedtime, her mother

would tuck her in tight and tell stories of princesses, star-catchers, and mermaids. Her mother would kiss her forehead before turning off the light, and Eden would drift off into a happy sleep. There would be no fears of monsters in closets or goblins under the bed.

Eden closed the curtains. Her mother's gloomy world twisted around in her mind as she changed into her pajamas, and the sketchbook's nightscapes whirled like wisps of lost memories when she turned off the light, pulled the quilt over her head, and faded off to sleep.

But then a nightmare bolted her awake.

Eden stumbled out of bed, quickly turning on the lamp on the nightstand. Slowly, she revisited slivers of the dream. She had been on a beach with black sand. A stormy ocean churned under a moonless sky full of stars. The beautiful woman from the sketchbook appeared, wearing a dress that floated around her as if she was underwater. But then the woman gripped Eden's shoulder, and sharp nails sank painfully into her skin.

The Witch of Everdark bent down and whispered in Eden's ear. "Been too long since a bright girl come here."

The witch had been vivid and terrifying, and Eden shivered away the memory of the nightmare.

It was just a bad dream, she thought. *It wasn't real.*

When her pulse lost its panic and returned to its normal speed, Eden carefully got back into bed, but she didn't turn off the light. She held the quilt tight under her chin. Sleep wasn't coming anytime soon.

CHAPTER FOUR

A Special Celebration

Eden woke up to laughter. The lingering threads of the nightmare had vanished in the sunshine. Muffled voices in the musical tone that she had begun to love drifted in pleasant waves to the guest room. Yawning, she trudged down the hallway to Aunt Susanna's bright kitchen.

"There go the sleepyhead," her great-aunt said. "Come here, let me introduce you."

Two teen boys and a woman sat at the kitchen table, and Eden quickly retreated. She was still in her pajamas and hadn't brushed her teeth yet. Plus, she had forgotten to put on her satin scarf last night, and her hair stuck out in all directions.

Eden tried to tame her curls with her hands. "I'm not presentable."

"Stop playing, girl. These your folks. You don't have to impress nobody." Aunt Susanna ushered her into the kitchen. "This my daughter, Cornelia. And those her sons, Memphis and Mercury."

She stared at the boys and their similar features, realizing they were twins. "Hello, I'm Eden." Her voice was formal, as if she were meeting strangers.

"Mama's told me so much about you." Cornelia stood up

and hugged her. "So happy I finally get to meet my cousin from Maryland."

"I got bacon, eggs, and biscuits. If these boys can save you some!" Aunt Susanna swatted a towel at Mercury, who had snatched another biscuit from the tray. Memphis shook his head, laughing at both of them.

Eden joined them at the large round table and chose a biscuit. Warm and powdery, it melted instantly in her mouth like a cloud of goodness.

"Good, ain't they?" Memphis stated. "Can't eat just one."

"Nothing like grandma's drop biscuits." Mercury grabbed two more from the tray. "Nice meeting you, Eden."

The boys got up and scrambled out to the front yard. Aunt Susanna sat at the kitchen table with a cup of coffee. She reached for Cornelia's hand and squeezed. Eden witnessed the strong mother-daughter bond and tried to ignore the sharp twist in her chest.

When she heard Uncle Willie's warm laugh, she stood up to investigate, peeking out the kitchen window. Memphis and Mercury stacked wood in the cargo bed of their grandfather's truck, and Eden's father was helping them.

"What's going on?" Eden asked.

"Oh, they taking more wood for cooking," Aunt Susanna said. "Last night, Willie set the fire pit, so they heading back to finish up."

Cornelia appeared beside her. "They're going up to Big Savannah. It's a large meadow farther north. Not far from Loretta Beach. It's where we put out our spread and have a good old time."

"Been doing it this way before I was born," Aunt Susanna said. "Sharing the blessings of the land. Celebrate instead of cry."

Eden ate two more drop biscuits before returning to the guest room. She paused to stare at the sketchbook but didn't open it. The nightmare had been muted by the sunny morning. She opened a drawer and selected a striped shirt and jeans. When she returned from the bathroom and dressed, she sat on the bed and rubbed her hands with pomade. Finger-combing her thick hair, she gathered the curls into a messy bun.

She picked up her mother's photograph from the nightstand and stared. It had been a morning ritual since the memorial service. Eden wanted to remember every detail of her mother's face, to never forget what she looked like. Natalie had reassured her that it would never happen, but it still didn't stop Eden's heart from racing at the thought. *What if I forget her?*

She wanted to remember everything. The laughter, the summer garden, and the love. She closed her eyes. Her mother had been in this room. Maybe some of the same air her mother had inhaled was still here in this space. Eden took a deep breath.

When Aunt Susanna knocked on the door, Eden's exhale came out in a yelp.

"Sorry, baby. Didn't mean to interrupt you," she said. "We're gon' start our way to Big Savannah. But first we have to go to the blessing at First Church."

Eden remembered the steeple among the trees. She stood up and nodded. "I'm ready."

. . .

Willow Hammock was alive with sound. Each house they passed on the road was filled with families on porches and in packed dirt yards. They hugged and spoke in the island language Eden yearned to understand.

"You're trying to figure out what everybody is saying?" her older cousin asked.

"Yes," Eden admitted.

"That's the saltwater in us," Cornelia said. "Though I guess I'm more freshwater these days now I'm on the mainland."

"Did you learn the language when you grew up here?" Eden asked.

"Learned it before anything else. It's a creole of African languages from the tribes that came here. Mixed with English, French, even some Spanish. I can teach you some words."

"I would like that," Eden said.

They joined a group that had gathered in front of First Church. The building was made of wood and painted white, with large front doors, a gabled roof, and stained glass windows. Aunt Susanna had told her the church was one of the first buildings that the free people of Safina Island had built in Willow Hammock.

"First Church was remodeled a few years ago," Cornelia told Eden. "Lewis Tailor grew up on the island. He's an architect now, and he came down from Atlanta to bless us with his talent."

There was a solemn silence before the church doors opened. Four men in overalls and straw hats bounded down the steps. Eden recognized both of her cousins, Leroy and Denero Gardener. They were followed by six women wearing patterned dresses of burgundy and yellow. Miss Melba and Little Betsy were in this group. Each woman had on matching head wraps in different styles. The men clapped their hands, and the women erupted in song.

"They're going to do a ring shout," Cornelia said. "To honor our ancestors."

The women danced counterclockwise in a circle while the men held the rhythm of the song with the strong cadence of claps and stomps. Eden didn't recognize the song, but she still felt the emotions in her bones, a connection that needed no explanation. These were her people, her culture, and her family.

When the ceremony was done, the residents of Willow Hammock traveled down the dirt road to Big Savannah. The early afternoon air was humid and a sheen of sweat covered Eden's skin.

She found her father under a cove of trees with Mercury and Memphis. Uncle Willie tended a fire pit layered with horizontal pipes that supported a chicken-wire grill. A splayed pig lay on top and spirals of gray smoke wafted in the air. Her great-uncle stoked the fire before covering the hole with tin shingles.

Eden toured tables full of crab and fish. Aunt Susanna gave her a plate of rice smothered in a spicy tomato broth full of onions, peppers, and sausage. Miss Melba gave her a glass of ginger tea, and Little Betsy offered okra soup. Her cousin Cornelia gave her a bowl of creamy grits covered with zesty brown gravy and jumbo shrimp.

By the end of the day, Eden and her father had sampled everything. They listened to the island families as they told stories of Willow Hammock's origin. The Gardener purchase of the land. The triumphs and the struggles. A living testimony to the deep history of her family. Eden wasn't sure what she had expected. But the food and fellowship were exactly what she had needed. All her worries disappeared. Eden hadn't disappointed her mother's family. Safina Island had welcomed her with open arms, but she still wondered why her mother never wanted to return to her birthplace.

CHAPTER FIVE

Full of Magic

Memphis and Mercury took Eden to Loretta Beach. Her feet sank into the sand, and the docile ocean waves foamed over her toes. Driftwood was scattered along the shore and ibis birds squawked above them.

Eden left her cousins at the surf to sit on a dune covered with beach grass. The sunset was behind her, and a deep relaxation seeped into her bones as she watched the sky dim into early dusk. Tendrils of the nightmare still lingered in Eden's memory, but now she was here experiencing the tranquility of Loretta Beach, which was so different from the haunting darkness of her mother's sketchbook. She pushed the ominous dream away and embraced the calm sound of the ocean.

An elderly woman approached, and Eden recognized her as Miss Nadine of the Brown family. She had joined her sisters, Little Betsy and Miss Melba, in the ring shout in front of First Church. No longer covered by a head wrap, the old woman's cottony hair blew in the breeze.

The island elder grumbled as she crouched low to find a comfortable spot on the dune, rejecting any of Eden's help. They sat in silence for several moments before the old woman spoke.

"Your mama used to sit and watch them waves for hours."

"You knew her?" Eden asked.

"Sure did. A firecracker, that one. Walked around Safina like she owned it. Girl always had one of them sketch pads with her."

Eden smiled thinking of her mother wandering the roads, meadows, and beaches. She could picture her studying the ocean and then moving a pencil across a blank page.

"I would have loved growing up here," Eden said. "It's so beautiful."

"That much true. Safina a gem like no other," Miss Nadine agreed. "And you just like your mama. Got that magic springing off your skin like new shine."

Heat rushed to Eden's face. The old woman had to be mistaken, because there wasn't anything buzzing off her skin. Especially not magic. Despite what Granny Alma had told her, being a Gardener didn't feel like an extra blessing. If anything, Eden felt doubly cursed. The block of ice was still heavy on her chest.

"I don't think there's any magic in me," she said.

Miss Nadine reached out with her calloused hands, touching Eden's knee. The old woman slowly nodded, as if confirming her statement. "Gardener girls been full of magic ever since they come across the water. Same shine live in you."

Eden looked into the elder's eyes, brown irises ringed with blue. "If you say there's magic in me, then I guess I have to believe you."

Miss Nadine pointed to the ocean. "Look ya! Our people lay at the bottom. Bones picked clean now. But some of us came on the land to see what it be."

Eden stared at the horizon. Hundreds of years ago, a ship

had crossed the water. White sails that carried the cargo of Eden's ancestors.

"Safina ain't truly our home, but we made it so. We started over and found new seeds to sow," the elder continued. "Look, I ain't a Gardener and I ain't marry one like my sisters, but they done did a lot for this land. All them blessed women doing the work. You and your mama come from that blood."

Eden's mother had told her years ago that the Gardener name was revered on the island. The family had protected the land and preserved its history. Being a descendant from such a bloodline had always made Eden proud, and now that she was seeing Safina Island with her own eyes, she wondered how her mother could have never returned to such a beautiful place.

"My mom went to the mainland and never came back," Eden said. "She left everything behind."

"Can't leave Safina behind," Miss Nadine said. "Your mama took it with her."

Eden felt the truth in the old woman's words. Her mother had brought Safina Island with her to the mainland. It had been evident in the summer garden. When the soil went fallow and was covered with frost, her mother told Eden that the flowers would return. A cycle of nature and life. Eden still wanted to believe in the hopeful words about returning blooms, but it seemed impossible now that her mother was gone.

Miss Nadine may have been right about taking the beauty of Safina Island to the mainland, but Eden knew that her mother had also left some things behind. A sketchbook full of cursed children and monstrous creatures. She wondered if Miss

Nadine knew about the dark images that had swum inside her mother's head.

"Did my mom ever show you any of her sketches?" Eden asked.

"One time she come to my house. Drew the sunflowers in my garden." Miss Nadine grinned at the memory. "Still got that one in a frame. Your mama was mighty talented. She sent Little Suzy a bunch of her fancy books, so I got them, too."

"My mom drew a lot of other things besides flowers." Eden paused. "She . . . she liked the night."

No recognition appeared on Miss Nadine's face. Maybe her mother hadn't shown anyone her creepy drawings. Maybe no one knew about her mother's affinity for the dark, but Eden wasn't quite convinced.

But before she could ask Miss Nadine more questions, her twin cousins called out to her as they walked up to the dune, their bare feet caked with sand.

"Getting late. We should head on back," Mercury said.

"Let me help you up, Miss Nadine." Memphis leaned down and helped the old woman to her feet.

Eden stood up and brushed off her jeans. The questions about her mother's sketchbook would have to wait. Before following her cousins back to Willow Hammock, Eden took one last look at the ocean's peaceful waves as the sun surrendered its last rays of light.

CHAPTER SIX
Island Stories

After a full day of festivities, the island folks and their families settled into their houses. Some of Eden's relatives had already said their goodbyes and returned to the mainland, while others lingered on screened porches.

By nightfall, Willow Hammock had grown quiet. Eden no longer heard musical voices or booming laughter. There was only the island breeze moving through the bottle trees and cricket night songs.

Her father and great-uncle had left earlier to ferry the last of the relatives to the mainland, and now they relaxed on the porch playing checkers. Aunt Susanna was in the kitchen washing dishes with her daughter, Cornelia. Her cousin's family was staying in one of the birdhouses for the night.

In the small guest room, Eden sat on the narrow bed. The sketchbook was still on the nightstand next to her mother's photograph. Although she hadn't opened it again, the creepy images had transferred from the warped pages and into her mind. Now in the evening stillness, the nightmare came back into focus. The moonless black beach and the stormy ocean. She shuddered as she remembered the witch sinking her sharp nails into her skin.

It was only a bad dream, Eden reminded herself.

Her thoughts were interrupted by a knock at the door, and Aunt Susanna poked her head in the doorway. "Mind some company?"

Eden nodded and her great-aunt entered the room and sat next to her on the bed.

"First full day on Safina. You met a lot of folks today. How you feel?"

"Tired, but not sleepy tired."

"I'm glad. Pure blessing to see family," her great-aunt said. "Memphis said y'all went to the beach."

"It was nice." Eden paused. "I talked with Miss Nadine for a while."

"Did you now?" Her great-aunt chuckled. "She don't leave the island much. Hope she didn't fill you up too much with her island stories."

Eden remembered the solid stare in the elder's eyes. The certainty of what the old woman had seen on her skin.

"She did say my mom had strong magic," Eden said. "Told me I was full of magic too."

"That don't surprise me none. She think we all got some kind of magic in us."

"You don't believe it?" Eden asked.

"Gardener girls are great, but we don't have no *real* magic. Oh, if I had that kind of power, the things I would do!" Aunt Susanna squeezed Eden's shoulders and laughed. "But some of us do have small blessings. Your granny could find lost things, but nothing more fancy than that. We mostly known for what we can do with the land. You see, these island roots keep us connected to our ancestors and the soil protects the bond."

"Miss Nadine said Safina is in our blood," Eden said.

"That much true," Aunt Susanna agreed, but then her eyes focused on the nightstand, and recognition appeared on her face. She leaned over and picked up the sketchbook. "See you done found your mama's dream book."

"Sorry," Eden said quickly. "I was in the closet and I saw the boxes—"

"No need to apologize," her great-aunt interrupted. "I was keeping those things for her."

"You thought she was coming back," Eden stated sadly.

"I did." Aunt Susanna opened the sketchbook, but she didn't seem disturbed by any of the drawings. "Your mama always did have a whole imagination."

"So those drawings are from . . . dreams?" Eden asked.

Her nightmare had felt real. The stormy ocean and black beach. The terror of the witch and her long, sharp nails.

"I reckon most of these are from dreams. Although I blame your granddaddy for some of the others," Aunt Susanna replied. "Before he left for the mainland, he told your mama the same island stories told to him."

Aunt Susanna pointed to the drawing of the monstrous black dog with the dagger teeth. "That there is a plat-eye. Created from victims of tragic deaths. You can find them near graveyards, but a splash of water keep them away."

Eden stared at the dog's mangled fur. She had doubts that something as simple as water could keep her safe from such a dangerous creature.

Her great-aunt turned to the drawing of the large bird with the sharp claws. "This Old Buzzard. Folks say he was a powerful god-spirit who took the skin of a man. Come to Safina to lay his tricks for harm. Got mighty rich from his evil deeds. Even the white man feared him. But when he tired of his human shell, folks say he returned to his true form and wait at the crossroads."

"What's the crossroads?" Eden asked.

"Crossroads is where you can speak with the dead and god-spirits," Aunt Susanna answered. "But nothing good come from speaking with Old Buzzard," her great-aunt went on. "Not unless you want eternal suffering and pain. Even if he give you what you want. Always a price to pay with his offer."

Aunt Susanna tutted her dislike as she turned more pages of the sketchbook. She didn't like the dark. Not like Eden's mother did. But she smiled when she saw the drawing of the black cat. "Your mama loved black cats."

"Are you sure?" Eden asked. "I don't think Mom liked cats at all."

"On Safina, they good luck. Folks say if a black cat cross your path, a life-changing event coming. You ever see a cat just stare off into space? They probably done seen a spirit. Folks even say black cats are godlike themselves and can travel between worlds."

Eden leaned over and stared at her mother's sketch of the black cat and its bright eyes. This drawing didn't create a chill up her spine like the plat-eye or Old Buzzard. The black cat gave her a mysterious comfort.

"What about the others?" Eden asked. "The ones of the children and the witch?"

Aunt Susanna shook her head. "Them the ones your mama claimed to see in her dreams."

"Did she ever tell you anything more about them?" Eden asked.

Aunt Susanna closed the sketchbook. "Listen, I'm going to tell you something, but you don't make it no show. Okay?"

Eden slowly nodded.

"Some folks on this island believe spirits stay to protect our blood kin. Show them the way when their time come. They believe a thin line separate the living world and the spirit world."

"Is Everdark the spirit world?" Eden asked.

"Your mama called it that," Aunt Susanna said. "But I never paid her no mind. Your mama was known to spin a story. I believe Everdark was something she made up for herself. She was mighty sad when your granddaddy left for the mainland."

Eden knew about her grandparents' divorce. How her grandfather had left Safina Island and never returned. He remained estranged and Eden had never met him. Neither Granny Alma nor her mother ever spoke of him. Underneath the gloom and danger in the sketchbook, there was grief. Sadness that cut like a knife, deep and dark. Eden knew this feeling well. But there was still something else that tugged at her, a familiarity she couldn't explain.

"So there's nothing in this book that's real?" she asked.

"There is one place." Her great-aunt opened the sketchbook again. "The Renata Mansion. Now that's real. It's on the south side of the island where all the white folks used to live."

Eden stared at the drawing of the mansion. Roots and leaves

crawled up its columns, covering the windows like a blindfold.

"Tomorrow, Willie can take you and your daddy for a look," her great-aunt continued. "The Spelling family let him do tours there."

Aunt Susanna placed the sketchbook on the nightstand, but there was still something else Eden needed to know.

"Aunt Susanna, can I ask you something else?"

"Sure. What you wanna ask?"

"My mom had an accident before she left the island. Do you know what happened?"

Aunt Susanna's smile faded and there was a slight alarm in her eyes. Only for a few seconds, but Eden noticed it.

"I wasn't here much during that time. I was on the mainland going to school," her great-aunt replied. "I just know your mama got hurt bad and then had to go to the mainland to heal."

"But she never came back," Eden said.

"I'm sorry, baby, that's all I know," Aunt Susanna said.

Eden's shoulders drooped in disappointment. Maybe it was as simple as her mother getting hurt and having to leave for the mainland. Maybe the sad memories kept her away.

Her mother had created Everdark as a coping mechanism. The sketches were figments of her imagination. There wasn't a mystery to be solved or more answers to find.

"Little Eden, pay no never mind to what you seen in your mama's book. Nothing can hurt you here. This land done soaked up all the bad. You safe." Eden's great-aunt stood up and kissed the top of Eden's head, leaving her alone in the wood-paneled guest room.

Eden changed into her pajamas and wrapped a satin scarf around her hair. Aunt Susanna didn't believe the Witch of Everdark in her mother's sketchbook was real, but something deep inside her couldn't shake a hidden truth. If the Renata Mansion was real, then couldn't Everdark be real too?

CHAPTER SEVEN

The Renata Mansion

After Sunday morning service at First Church, Eden sat between her father and Uncle Willie in his pickup truck. Well fed with Aunt Susanna's skillet-fried chicken, cornbread, and red peas, they left Willow Hammock and drove south on a sandy road. Dust floated up in waves, and sunlight leaked through the fresh leaves of cypress trees. Eden couldn't see the ocean yet, but she could smell salt in the air.

She had experienced a night of restful sleep. A nightmare hadn't bolted her awake. Maybe Aunt Susanna was right after all. Everdark wasn't real. Maybe traveling to the Renata Mansion would help Eden realize that there was nothing to fear.

This land done soaked up all the bad, Aunt Susanna had said.

Uncle Willie made a turn onto a paved road, its smoothness a stark difference from the rugged path they had traveled. Eden leaned around her father, eager to view the surroundings on the south side of the island.

"All of this privately owned?" Dr. Leopold asked.

"That be right. Everything still in the Spelling family name," Uncle Willie said. "But the state wants to buy it."

"What would they do with it?" Eden asked.

"Too much history to let it waste. Reckon they would open

the mansion up for visits like they do other places on the south side," Uncle Willie replied.

Eden knew Safina Island had deep roots. Indigenous tribes and Spanish missionaries. French land surveyors and enslaved West Africans. But the Spellings had left the biggest mark. Even the Gardeners couldn't overshadow their legacy.

"The family doesn't live in the mansion?" Eden asked.

"Been long time since a Spelling lived here proper. Empty right now, but for the right price, they rent it out for weddings."

Dr. Leopold frowned. "Why would anyone have a wedding here? Isn't the mansion built up from the old plantation house?"

Uncle Willie nodded. "Them Spellings was the ones who brung us here. They lived in that Big House until it burned down during the Civil War."

Eden remained quiet. She hated hearing about the plight of her ancestors. Unlike the block of ice that sat heavy on her chest, she experienced a different feeling for this. It was a scalding brew in the pit of her stomach. She didn't know how to dispel the resentment directed at a family forever linked with hers through the legacy of chattel slavery. She wondered how the Spelling descendants felt about their long enslaver history on Safina Island, isolated and surrounded by the ocean.

The truck filled with silence as they passed a vast manicured lawn where island trees cast shifting shadows. Eden's skin tingled with nerves. Uncle Willie kept driving along the paved road until the Renata Mansion emerged from the lush foliage.

Eden followed her father out of the truck, and they traveled down a seashell path to the front of the mansion. Dr. Leopold stopped at an empty fountain filled with old leaves. A marble angel stood at its center, cracked with age.

Surrounded by palmetto trees and live oaks, the Renata Mansion matched her mother's sketch perfectly. Solid white and full of archways, the entrance boasted tall, ornate glass doors that glinted in the afternoon sunlight. Eden realized the mansion was actually three buildings connected by enclosed walkways with arched windows. The main structure had four thick columns that supported an extravagant portico. Several wrought-iron chairs and tables were positioned on both sides of the entry doors.

"Charles Spelling finished building this mansion in 1926," Uncle Willie said. "Right on the ruins of his great-granddaddy's Big House. He was a newlywed, so he named it after his wife. Even kept the original tabby foundations and walls."

"What's tabby?" Eden asked.

"It's a process, you see," Uncle Willie said. "You burn oyster shells for the lime base. Then you mix in sand and water. Put in more oyster shells until it look like cement. That make it strong enough for hurricanes like the one in 1809. Most ruins on Safina was made with tabby."

Dr. Leopold wandered to the north wing of the mansion to survey the architecture, but Eden walked up the stairs and stood in front of the entry doors. They towered over her, and she fingered the floral iron design protecting the glass. Peering inside, she saw a great room with high ceilings supported by thick wood beams. White sheets covered furniture, and the fireplace mantel was bare. Although sunlight filtered through the vast space, the mansion was eerie and dark.

Then she saw movement underneath one of the covered tables. A gray, mottled foot appeared from under the sheet. Eden squinted, pressing closer until her nose smushed against the cool door, and the bruised foot jerked back under the table.

It's a trick of the light, she thought.

But the sheet moved again, a slight wobble as if something underneath was trying to stay hidden but failing. Eden's heart sped up in her chest. There was something inside the mansion. When a hand landed on her shoulder, she gasped.

"Didn't mean to spook you, Little Eden," Uncle Willie said. "Mansion locked, so we can't go inside."

Eden's fingers felt stiff as she held them against her fluttering heart. She didn't want to enter the mansion. A cold warning settled between her shoulder blades. She moved away from the doors and quickly joined her father on the grand lawn.

Uncle Willie continued to show them the mansion's grounds, including a greenhouse now overgrown and reunited with nature. Her grandmother had told her it was after freedom that the family had chosen Gardener as their last name. It was what they had been known for on the island, because there wasn't anything their family couldn't grow. *Never let anyone tell you that we were unworthy,* Granny Alma had said. *We were prized for our knowledge of the land, and that's why we were enslaved.*

Now they were in a courtyard behind the mansion where two large palmetto trees loomed over a solarium. Inside a large arched window, a mermaid sculpture held a mirror, her tail forever frozen in midswish. In the distance beyond the seashell paths, the ocean met the sky.

"Back in the day, mansion had an indoor pool," Uncle Willie said. "Charles Spelling would take morning swims."

"I can only imagine how this place looked back in its prime," Dr. Leopold said.

"Days of wine and roses," Uncle Willie said. "For them, anyway. But Charles Spelling didn't see too many of those."

"What happened to him?" Dr. Leopold asked.

"Died mysteriously in 1936. Folks say his wife laid a trick on him."

Dr. Leopold huffed in doubt. "You don't believe that, do you?"

Eden had heard the island stories of cursed deaths. In certain hands, the knowledge of the natural world could harm as well as heal. It all depended upon the intent. But Eden also knew her father didn't believe in this type of power. He was a man of science, not magic.

"Safina got many secrets," Eden's great-uncle said. "Laying tricks is one of them. But ain't nothing to talk about now. What's done been done."

Uncle Willie led them out of the courtyard to the mansion's beach. He pointed to smaller sister islands in the distance. Over the years they had been home to navy forts, quarantine hospitals, and smaller fishing hammocks. Even once the hidden lair of a famous pirate. He told them about the erosion and how parts of Safina Island would eventually succumb to the ocean.

"Don't nothing last forever," he said.

When the tour of the grounds had ended, Dr. Leopold followed Uncle Willie back to the pickup truck, but Eden lingered in front of the empty fountain. She stared at the Renata Mansion, majestic in its towering presence but fading in its glory.

A black cat bounded onto the grand lawn, moving in confident strides. Crossing Eden's path, it settled on the portico in front of the entry doors and gazed at her with an eerie focus, its goldenrod eyes reflecting the sunlight.

The black cat then slowly turned its gaze toward the mansion's doors. Peering inside, the cat pounced its paws against the glass. Then it stood rigid and hissed, back hunched and fur puffed. Eden's heartbeat pulsed loudly in her ears. She remembered that black cats could see spirits.

"Little Eden, you okay?"

She turned to find Uncle Willie in front of his truck, waving his hands in the air.

"Been calling your name. Everything all right?"

A sheen of sweat now coated Eden's forehead. She shivered, as if she had broken a fever. Eden had been spooked by the black cat. Or rather, what it had also seen inside the mansion.

She returned the wave to her great-uncle. "I'm fine."

When Eden turned to look back at the Renata Mansion, the black cat was gone.

CHAPTER EIGHT

Fading Legacy

The visit to the Renata Mansion gave Eden too many things to grapple with, and she tried to manage the growing fear that the place was haunted. The reaction from the black cat also made it hard to ignore what she had seen through the glass doors.

Uncle Willie drove them to other locations on the island. Ruins of another plantation, an old sugar mill, and a defunct seafood cannery. They even visited indigenous shell rings that archeologists dated as being over four thousand years old.

Dr. Leopold asked most of the questions during these tours while Eden remained silent. The history of Safina Island was immense, but it was only the Renata Mansion that occupied her thoughts.

When they returned to Willow Hammock in the early evening, Aunt Susanna had invited family and neighbors to the house. They were settled around the kitchen table, voices intertwining like a small orchestra. Little Betsy and Miss Melba had come with their husbands. Members of the Brown and Tailor families from down the road had also been invited, including Miss Nadine, who watched Eden closely with her blue-rimmed eyes.

Can she see any magic in me today? Eden wondered.

She had already said goodbye to her relatives after Sunday service at First Church. Cornelia and the twins had returned to the mainland, but Eden had promised she would keep in touch.

Dr. Leopold devoured another plate of skillet-fried chicken that Aunt Susanna had made fresh for him, but Eden declined the offer for more food because her stomach was clenched in tight knots.

"Y'all hear about Deborah's son?" Little Betsy's husband asked the group.

"What he done now?" Aunt Susanna asked.

"He selling the family land," Miss Melba's husband answered.

"What a shame. His mama ain't even been in the grave a full season," Uncle Willie said. "He shoulda come to us first."

"Are a lot of people selling their land?" Dr. Leopold asked.

"We see it sometime. The north side of Safina is either Gardener land or heir property," Aunt Susanna said. "Sheldon's mama was the last of the Hope family living, so he don't need no blessing from us."

"Don't wanna live here, so he wanna be rid of it," Little Betsy's husband said in an irritated tone.

What had been a joyful conversation full of laughter was now stagnant and resigned, as if someone had turned down the wick in a lantern. Eden squirmed nervously in her chair.

"It's the taxes," Uncle Willie told Eden's father. "That's why a lot of folks sell. They keep going up. We try to help as much as we can, but sometimes folks just want out."

"Tate Bonner bought a nice double-wide for his mama,"

Miss Melba volunteered in a light voice, as if to change the subject. "Should be coming soon. Heard it real nice."

"Is it easier to get mobile homes instead of building a house?" Dr. Leopold asked.

Uncle Willie nodded. "State got so many regulations. Easier to bring one already done. Either way, property taxes still got to be paid."

Eden didn't know if Granny Alma or her mother had sent any money to support the Gardener land. She worried about the possible hardships for Uncle Willie, Aunt Susanna, and the rest of her relatives.

"I don't have a job yet, but I can give money for taxes when I get one," she volunteered.

Dr. Leopold touched Eden's shoulder and the rest of the table looked at her, which made Eden want to disappear. But Aunt Susanna beamed with pride and the others nodded their approval.

"We can definitely help with the taxes," her father added.

"Mighty fine of y'all," Aunt Susanna said. "We tend to get by from tours and the birdhouses. We also get money from our crops and fishery, too. But we welcome any extra money to keep this land in our names."

The table murmured their agreement, and the muscles in Eden's jaw relaxed. Lightness returned to the room when Aunt Susanna brought out three different pies. Eden listened to stories of pranks and adventures. Her family had aged along with the island, and seeing all the brown faces full of wisdom, Eden realized Willow Hammock could easily disappear when these elders passed on. She was one of the few left who needed to keep the legacy of her family from fading away.

Don't nothing last forever, Uncle Willie had said.

But Eden didn't want to think about the future, and she didn't want to dwell in the past. There was too much pain and sad memories. Eden decided she would focus on the present moment in Aunt Susanna's kitchen, with the living relatives who loved her.

She also decided she would try her best to let go of everything that troubled her. The fear of the Renata Mansion and the strange black cat. Her mother's sketchbook and its morbid darkness. She only had one day left on the island, and Eden wanted to cherish her time with the Gardener family.

Night swooped onto Safina Island and shrouded Willow Hammock in darkness. Stars winked behind thick clouds, and ocean waves crested against the shore. Marsh grasses swayed in the evening breeze. Neighbors and relatives had returned to their houses, bright lanterns showing them the way.

Eden helped Aunt Susanna wash and dry the dishes while Uncle Willie and her father spoke softly on the porch, their voices filtering through the open kitchen window.

"Safina been good to you today?" Aunt Susanna asked.

"There's a lot here," Eden said.

"Safina got a lot of layers." Aunt Susanna squeezed a wet towel and placed it to dry over the sink. "What you think of the mansion?"

Eden didn't want to talk about the Renata Mansion and

how it had jostled fears and doubts, but she didn't want her great-aunt to know that she was anxious about the place.

"It was big. We couldn't go inside." She paused. "I saw a black cat."

Aunt Susanna cocked her head. "Is that so?"

A nervous itch crept up Eden's neck and she quickly scratched her skin. "Do you know who it belongs to?"

"Miss Nadine got a black cat," her great-aunt answered. "Did it have a red collar?"

When Eden shook her head, Aunt Susanna shrugged her shoulders. "Probably a stray then."

"I remember what you said about black cats," Eden said. "Is . . . is the Renata Mansion haunted?"

"I reckon this whole island haunted," her great-aunt answered. "So many things done happened on Safina. Especially in that house. Wouldn't surprise me none if spirits roam there, but that ain't nothing for you to worry about."

Aunt Susanna didn't seem concerned that the Renata Mansion was haunted. But the black cat had hissed, as if whatever it saw was evil or dangerous. Eden pushed the disturbing thought away. There was no need to worry about the mansion. She would never walk inside its walls.

When she returned to the guest room, Eden pulled out pens and stationery. She had promised Natalie that she would send her a letter. Crossing her legs on the bed, Eden wrote about the island's culture and food and the experience of meeting her relatives, but she didn't mention anything else. She didn't tell her best friend about the creepy sketchbook full of her mother's morbid imagination. Instead Eden wrote about Safina Island's beauty, which was one of the things that she knew as fact.

In the morning, she would ask Uncle Willie to take her to the post office at Marien Landing to send the letter off, although she would already be back in Maryland before it arrived.

After taking a hot shower, she changed into her pajamas and opened the curtains to stare at the darkness of the woods. The island looked different at night. She thought of the moon draping the Renata Mansion in silver light, and whatever was hidden underneath the covered table now roaming free.

Eden shuddered and shook the scary images from her head. Burrowing into bed, she turned off the lamp and pulled the quilt over her head. Her muscles sighed in relief after a long day of touring the island. Her eyelids slowly grew heavy and she fell into a deep sleep.

CHAPTER NINE

A Dark Dream

The hallway was dim, and Eden fumbled through the darkness. The dirt floor was cool on her bare feet. She blinked several times to try to get her eyes to adjust to the gloom, pressing her hands against the walls. She found several locked doors, the splintered wood rough on her fingertips.

I'm in a dream, she thought.

Eden had fallen asleep, but her awareness was keen. She wasn't on the moonless beach but somewhere else. Underground in a cellar or a basement. A hidden place.

The musky undertone filled her nose, a scented memory of her mother's summer garden after a heavy rain. Taking a shallow breath, she wandered in the damp dark. A weak source of light was ahead of her, and she moved toward it.

But she stopped when she heard whispers.

The murmurs hummed from behind the closed doors and through jagged cracks in the walls. Eden couldn't understand the distorted words. The whispers elevated into eager chants.

Dread loomed in Eden's chest as she continued to travel to the end of the hallway. She stood at the bottom of a staircase. Looking upward, Eden found the source of light that sliced through the darkness. There was a lantern on the top step, its flickering flame bright. A deep warning sparked inside Eden, and she moved back into the gloom.

The doors in the hallway trembled on their hinges, frames buckling until they split open and crashed to the floor in plumes of dust. Eden coughed as wind whipped sharp and cold. Dark shadows rushed toward her, and hands tugged on her pajamas. She tried to break free, but there were too many of the vaporous shapes. Overwhelmed, Eden closed her eyes and pressed her hands against her ears to block out the desperate pleas.

"Stop!" she finally cried.

The dirt floor shifted under Eden's feet, and she slowly opened her eyes.

She was now on a beach. The black sand glinted in the silver light of a full moon and the night sky sparkled with stars. Ocean waves gently rolled onto the shore. She was no longer in the hidden place. Eden sighed in relief, but then realized she wasn't alone.

A little girl wearing a high-necked dress was on the beach, her indigo skin shimmering under the moon.

Eden swallowed her unease. "Hello?"

The little girl didn't respond.

"Can you hear me?"

The little girl still didn't answer. She hadn't even blinked, but her bright eyes glowed in the darkness.

It's only a dream, Eden remembered.

She had stopped the shadows from tormenting her in the hidden place. Maybe in this dreamworld, she held power.

"Speak," Eden commanded.

As if she were a marionette on a string, the little girl reacted and spoke in a raspy voice. "Best leave now."

Eden moved closer and saw that the little girl's dress was ripped like a wind-torn flag and her leather boots were old and stretched.

"Why?" Eden asked. "Is someone coming?"

The little girl's legs wobbled on the sand as she took two steps back. "Best leave while you still can," she repeated. "This ain't no place for a bright girl."

"Is this Everdark?"

The little girl answered by slowly raising her hand; the sleeve of her torn dress was discolored with stains. She pointed to the woods in the distance. "Run."

A sliver of cold traveled up Eden's spine as the little girl's hand started to tremble. Eden searched the beach. She found no one else. They were alone.

"Tell me who's coming? Is it the witch?"

"Run!" the little girl suddenly screamed. "Run!"

Eden stumbled away as the ground shifted again. The beach disappeared and now she was surrounded by crumbling stone pillars. Heavy fog hovered in the air and a panic crawled up Eden's legs and settled into her stomach when she realized she was in a cemetery.

The ground was covered with dead leaves, and she walked carefully around the tombstones. Broken clocks and cracked plates leaned against some of the grave markers while others had smaller mementos. A spiked black fence enclosed the cemetery like a gloomy prison.

Clouds covered the moon and Eden squinted in the darkness. The dread slowly built inside her again as she searched for the gate entrance. In the heavy silence, Eden maneuvered around decaying markers of the dead.

A low growl came from behind her. Trembling, she slowly turned around. The hulking dark shape had pointy ears and red, glowing eyes. Eden instantly recognized this creature and stared at the plat-eye in horror.

The monstrous dog growled again, revealing its sharp teeth. Eden searched frantically for a way out and spotted the gate entrance. But then she remembered she was in a dream. There was no need for her to run. She held all the power in this dreamworld. There was nothing to fear.

"Go away!" Eden shouted. "Now!"

The plat-eye didn't heed her command. Prowling closer, its growls grew deeper with menace. Eden stumbled backward, tripping over a broken tombstone.

"Leave me alone!" she shrieked.

The monstrous dog still advanced toward her, and Eden cried out in fear. If she had any power in this dream, she had already used it up. Her commands were no longer working.

"Wake up," Eden whispered frantically. "Wake up."

The plat-eye lunged toward her, forcing Eden to run. She jumped over broken pillars as the cemetery blurred in her vision. When her bare feet slipped on the dead leaves, Eden tumbled to the ground and fell into an open grave.

She whimpered in terror as the plat-eye loomed over the edge, its dagger teeth gleaming in the gloom. Eden scrambled to her feet, but it was too late. The monstrous dog leaped, and she felt its full weight on her.

Eden bolted up in bed, her breath caught in her chest. She was back in the wood-paneled guest room. Hands trembling, she turned on the light on the nightstand.

She had been in Everdark. She felt the recognition deep in her bones. The sketchbook wasn't filled with images from her mother's imagination. Everdark had felt as real as the Renata Mansion. Her mother had been to this place, and now she had been there too.

CHAPTER TEN

Return of the Black Cat

Eden sat bleary-eyed at her great-aunt's kitchen table. She had eaten a drop biscuit, but now it felt like a cold stone in her stomach.

Her father finished eating the eggs on his plate as he chatted with Uncle Willie. "Where should we go today?"

"We can go down south to Marien Landing," Uncle Willie said. "Marine institute open today."

Dr. Leopold nodded and then took a sip of his coffee. "Eden, we can see if they have any postcards. Didn't you want to send one to Natalie?"

Her father's voice sounded far away, as if blocked by a thick curtain. She stared at him, trying to understand the words he had spoken.

"You don't look too good, Little Eden," Uncle Willie said.

"I'm just tired," she replied.

Aunt Susanna's brows knitted together in concern. "Maybe you should stay here and get some rest."

Dr. Leopold quickly moved forward, touching Eden's forehead. "No fever, but you don't look well. Are you sure you're okay?"

"Maybe y'all wore the girl out yesterday on all them tours," Aunt Susanna suggested.

Eden hadn't gone back to sleep. After she had calmed down from the lucid dream, she had found black sand in her bed. Her feet were dirty, as if she had been outside.

She had also opened the sketchbook. Her mother's sketches were now familiar because of the dream. The collection of hands reaching out in the darkness was from the hallway in the hidden place. The little girl she had met on the beach was also there, with her luminous eyes. Most disturbing was the plat-eye who had cornered her in the cemetery. Her mother had drawn them all accurately.

Eden had never believed in magic. Not magic that was dangerous and dark. Yet even with the looming dread that now wrapped around her, she was still drawn to its mystery.

Everdark is real, she thought.

"Eden?" Dr. Leopold's voice brought her back to the bright kitchen.

"I'm not sick." Eden stifled a yawn. "But I'm tired."

"Y'all head out to Marien Landing," Aunt Susanna said. "Little Eden can stay with me."

Uncle Willie stood up from the kitchen table. "Best we get a move on. We can go the back way so we can drive by the Dublin River. If we lucky, may see a gator or two."

Dr. Leopold chuckled nervously. "Let's hope we're not that lucky."

When her father and great-uncle left, Eden went into the den and sat on the sofa. After a few moments, Aunt Susanna brought her a pillow and a quilt.

"Need to travel down the road for a quick spell," she said.

"Need to talk with Miss Nadine about planting season."

"I can go with you," Eden offered.

Aunt Susanna shook her head. "You can barely keep your eyes open, baby. Besides, I won't be long."

Her great-aunt wrapped her up in the quilt and kissed her forehead. Eden closed her eyes after Aunt Susanna went out the back door, but no sleep came to her. The truth of Everdark was burning on her skin, keeping her from rest. After tossing and turning, she rose from the sofa.

Eden wanted answers about this spirit world. She wondered why her mother had never told her about the dark place that dwelled in her dreams.

Putting on her sneakers, she wandered into the backyard. She found two vast plots of upturned earth that filled the air with a rich aroma. Soon the plots would be planted with the seeds of the summer season. There would be tomatoes, okra, and corn. Aunt Susanna's flower garden showcased spring with azaleas and tulips. Later there would be summer flowers. Hyacinths, bluebells, and lily of the valley.

The chickens strutted on the soft-packed dirt, plucking at the ground, while the goats frolicked around the yard, their small bells clanging softly. White sheets on a laundry line blew in the island breeze. Eden sat on the back porch step and stared into the woods.

A flicker of a tail caught her attention, and then a dark shape emerged as it prowled among the resurrection ferns.

Eden felt a surge of warmth on the back of her neck when she saw the black cat. The same reaction she had when she saw it at the Renata Mansion. A deep feeling of recognition.

The black cat had disappeared from view, but when Eden spotted its tail again, she stood up and walked past the plowed land to the edge of the woods.

Maybe Aunt Susanna was right, and the black cat was a stray. On this island, it could easily survive in the wild. But there was something else that tugged at Eden. Her great-aunt also said black cats could see spirits and even travel between worlds. Eden's mother had drawn one in her sketchbook.

Eden walked slowly into the woods, the goats and chickens giving background noise. The canopy of the island trees provided natural shade. The ground was soft and slightly damp, reminding Eden of the marshes that lay farther north.

She scanned the woods for the black cat, but only the wind moved through the island trees like a lazy sigh, and morning sunlight broke out in patches on the ground.

Eden spotted the black cat's tail again among the resurrection ferns, twitching in the air. She followed it as it moved and darted, hunting some unseen prey. The black cat was hard to follow, but Eden kept pace with it. But then she lost it again in the underbrush, and she frowned in disappointment.

Turning back, she was surprised at how far she had traveled from her great-aunt's house. It was barely within view, the mint-green paint peeking out among the cypress and pine trees.

Eden surveyed her surroundings. The woods were bright and soothing. Her great-aunt had promised that there was nothing to fear on the island. She wasn't in a dark dream but in the real world. She was safe.

An area of the woods caught her eye. A slash of darkness that looked out of place. Eden squinted, thinking it could be a trick of the light, but the unusual dimness held.

Eden slowly approached and realized it was a jagged gash of darkness, as if ripped open with a knife. Then her eyes widened, because the opening revealed a night sky.

She held her breath as she moved around to the other side of the jagged gash. It instantly disappeared and Eden only saw the woods and her great-aunt's house in the distance. But when she returned to the front of the opening, it appeared again. The dark world she saw through it was a stark contrast to the bright morning around her.

Eden wondered if this was where the black cat had gone. Had it disappeared into this world? Why could Eden see this sliver of night in the woods?

It's magic, she thought.

For several moments, Eden stood mesmerized by the space that defied all logic. Here within the bright morning of Safina Island was another world.

Eden had thought that Everdark could only be accessed through dreams, but maybe she had been wrong. She moved so close to the jagged gash that she could feel the cool wind brushing her skin. This dark world was speaking to her and inviting her to enter, but she hesitated.

She remembered what her mother had drawn and what she had experienced in her dreams. The beautiful witch's sharp nails sinking into her skin. The weight of the plat-eye on her chest.

Eden stepped away and looked back at Aunt Susanna's

house. The right thing to do was to go back and lie down on the sofa. Wrap herself up in her great-aunt's quilt and forget about what she had seen. Tomorrow she would leave the island and go back to her life in Maryland. She would go back to her grief, and the heavy loss of her mother. But if she walked away, would she regret it? Eden bit her lip. Magic was real, and it had revealed itself to her. She wondered if this was the same spirit world her mother had drawn in the sketchbook, the one she had visited in her dreams. If she traveled to this world, could she speak with the dead?

Eden's curiosity pulled her back to the jagged opening, and she stared again at the dark world as a deep longing blossomed in her chest.

A small peek, she thought. *One quick look.*

Eden moved closer to the sliver of night. One foot edged to the opening, while the other pressed firmly to the ground. Eden peered inside. She could smell the salt of the ocean and saw similar island trees in the darkness. Then coldness brushed her cheeks and an instant dread alarmed her senses.

She jerked away from the jagged gash, but there was no longer any morning light. Eden turned to face her great-aunt's house, but it was gone. Her eyes widened in shock. The night sky was above her and she stood in the middle of a wild, untouched place.

A panic crawled up her legs and Eden bolted through the woods. She didn't know where she was going, but nothing else mattered in this moment. She ran between skinny trunks of pines and cypress, dodging live oaks with outstretched branches that hung close to the ground. Spanish moss brushed her neck like spiderwebs. Eden let out an anxious cry.

When she finally escaped the woods, she was at the edge of a beach. Eden followed the sound of the ocean. The black beach lay in front of her, stormy waves rolling against its shore. On the horizon, lightning pulsed inside dark clouds.

This isn't a dream, she thought.

Eden had crossed the thin line between the spirit world and the living world. She was in Everdark.

CHAPTER ELEVEN

The Moonless Beach

Eden didn't know if she had been crying for minutes or hours, but the tears had finally stopped and now she sat on the black beach, watching the waves through damp eyelashes.

She wiped her face with the T-shirt she had put on in the bright light of morning and shivered in the cold. The shorts she wore gave no warmth, and goose bumps covered her legs. Black, gritty sand had found its way into her sneakers. She held her growling stomach. Aunt Susanna's drop biscuit was long gone.

Eden turned to look at the woods and wondered if she could find her way back to Willow Hammock. Maybe in this dark spirit world she would find a bright sliver of sunshine that could take her back to Safina Island. But she was so tired and so cold. She didn't want to get lost in the dark. It would be safer to stay here on the beach.

In her dreams, Everdark had a moon-drenched night sky. But now it was dreary, and approaching storm clouds covered the bright stars.

Tears pooled in her eyes as she thought of her father. He would be so worried, and Aunt Susanna would be frantic when she returned and found only an empty sofa and a discarded quilt.

They wouldn't even know where to look. They wouldn't know to go into the woods and find the jagged gash that opened to another world. She wasn't even sure if they would be able to see it.

Eden had made the wrong choice. She should have never looked. Her curiosity had brought her to this spirit world. No one was coming for her, and no one would find her. A rush of new tears trailed down her cheeks.

In the distance, a twinkle of light caught her attention. Something was moving toward her. She tried to focus on the shape, but it was too far away. But when Eden blinked, she saw the shape of a person walking on the beach. Then she blinked again, and the figure appeared even closer, flickering in the darkness.

Eden stood up, a fresh fear gripping her. It was a woman carrying a lantern. The feeling of dread crept up her neck as she remembered last night's dream. In the hidden place, there had been a lantern at the top of the stairs, and an inner knowing had told her that it was dangerous. In the dream she had moved away, but here on the empty beach there was nowhere to go.

When she blinked again, the woman materialized right in front of her. Eden stumbled backward.

The woman's deep-indigo skin shimmered with tiny stars. She wore a high-necked blouse, and her long skirt billowed in the breeze. Thick hair wavered from the woman's face in long cottonlike tufts.

Her mother's watercolor drawings hadn't been able to capture the true essence of the Witch of Everdark. Here on the moonless beach, she was easily the most beautiful woman Eden had ever seen.

The witch raised her lantern and examined Eden's face. "What we got here?"

When Eden didn't answer, the witch moved closer. "A Gardener girl done crossed my path." The witch leaned in and sniffed Eden's skin. "Never heard of y'all being empty husks. Some things done changed, I see."

Standing rigid, Eden glanced at the woods. Her legs itched to run. The woods were now a safe haven. An avenue of escape.

The witch followed her gaze, her eyes glinting in the darkness. "Woods not safe at night for a bright girl like you."

"I'm lost." Eden finally found her voice. "Can you tell me how to get back to Willow Hammock?"

The witch's mouth curled into a cruel smile. "Why you wanna go back?"

"I don't belong here." Eden trembled. "I . . . I came here by accident."

The witch stopped smiling. When she tossed her long hair over her shoulder, Eden saw the witch's black nails. Long and sharp. Panic rose in Eden's chest, a bright bloom of terror.

"Gardener girls don't come here by accident," the witch said. "No matter. Even though you ain't got no shine, I can find use for a bright girl like you."

Thunder rumbled in the distance. Eden stood rigid as the witch circled, stopping right behind her. Eden's breath quickened in panic. The witch wasn't going to help her. If anything, she planned to hurt Eden, or worse.

When she lurched to run, the witch caught her in a tight grasp. "No need to fight me now. Hold still."

She whimpered as the witch caressed her arm. Cold breath brushed against Eden's ear. "I always wanted another daughter."

Waves crashed against the shore, and the roll of thunder loomed closer. A storm was coming. Eden cried out as the witch's grip tightened around her arm, the sharp nails piercing her skin. Ice poured into her veins and blackness crept into Eden's vision.

Her breathing turned shallow, and Eden could no longer fight what was happening to her. The rawness of the pain made her weak, and the will to escape leaked away.

Eden finally surrendered and fell into darkness.

CHAPTER TWELVE

Bright Girl

E den woke up in a bed and labored to a sitting position. Her head felt heavy, as if filled with stones. At her bedside, two girls with starry indigo skin stared at her. The older girl frowned, and the younger one widened her eyes. Both were in old-fashioned party dresses with long pearl necklaces. Eden looked down and saw that she wore a nightgown. The lace collar scratched against her neck.

"You 'wake?" the little girl asked.

Eden scrambled away from them, bumping into a nightstand, where a stained-glass lamp wobbled.

"You done scared her." The older girl scowled at the younger one.

Eden scanned the surroundings of the room. A gold-plated vanity and a silk-covered chair nestled in the corner. A large mahogany wardrobe faced the bed, and elegant wallpaper showcased palm fronds. The style was from another time period.

"Where am I?" Eden asked.

"In the mansion," the little girl answered.

"Where's the witch?"

The girls exchanged nervous looks with each other. When the older girl moved forward, Eden picked up the lamp from the nightstand.

"Put that down. We ain't gon' hurt you," she said.

"You safe," the little girl added.

Eden stared at the younger girl. She had been in her dream on the black beach—the spirit who had told her to run. But she looked different now. Her dress wasn't torn and ruined, but her eyes were still deep and luminous. She showed no recognition of Eden.

The older girl looked like the one her mother had drawn in the sketchbook, but she didn't have tight coils twisted up in a bun. Instead, her hair was pressed and styled in long ringlets.

Eden slowly placed the lamp on the nightstand. "Who are you?"

The older girl let out an irritated sigh. "We should be asking you that."

"My name Netty." The little girl pointed at the older one. "Her name Grace."

Grace frowned at Netty for speaking, but then turned back to Eden. "Why you here?"

"It was an accident!" Eden cried. "I don't want to be here!"

The little girl glanced at the door. "You need to be quiet. Mother Mary don't like shouting."

Netty seemed to be the most helpful of the two girls. Eden took a deep breath before speaking again. "I'm sorry. I'm just upset. My name's Eden. Who's Mother Mary?"

"This her mansion," Grace answered. "She the one who found you."

"She always go out at night," Netty added.

"Is this the Renata Mansion?" Eden asked.

Netty wrinkled her nose, as if she smelled something sour. "Mother Mary don't like it when you call it that."

"Is . . . is she the Witch of Everdark?"

"She don't like it when you call her that neither," Grace said.

The girls continued to stare at her. They didn't seem as creepy as they did in her mother's sketchbook. If anything, Grace seemed irritated and Netty looked worried.

She shifted closer to the girls. "Am I . . . dead?"

"You bright as can be," Grace sneered. "Nothing good happen when a bright girl show up."

"That ain't true," Netty said.

"Nobody care what you think," Grace snapped.

"Can you help me?" Eden asked the girls.

"Help you what?" Grace grumbled.

"Help me get out of here," Eden said. "I need to get back to Willow Hammock. Do you know where that is?"

"We ain't helping you do nothing," Grace replied. "You the one who came here. We ain't ask for your company."

"I want you to stay." Netty sat on the bed. "You so bright and pretty."

Eden looked down at her hands, which were still the dark brown that they had always been. No one would ever consider her light-skinned. "Bright" had to mean something different here.

A bright girl is a living girl, she realized.

"Do you know the way to Willow Hammock?" Eden asked the little girl.

Netty glanced at Grace and then rose from the bed. "It ain't allowed."

"It can be our secret." Eden hesitated. "You can pretend you had nothing to do with it—"

"We done told you. You ain't getting no help from us," Grace interrupted. "We up here to watch you. Not help you leave. This what you get for coming here."

Grace grabbed Netty's hand and marched toward the door. The little girl turned back to look at Eden with eyes full of regret.

"Wait!" Eden said. "I'm sorry. Wait!"

Grace pushed Netty into the hallway. "We was only supposed to watch you until you woke up." The older girl gave one last frown before leaving the room.

Eden scrambled out of bed, running to the door, but found it locked, the crystal knob slick in her sweaty hand.

She whirled and ran to the windows. The bedroom was on the second floor in the mansion's north wing, facing the courtyard. Two grand palmetto trees towered over the solarium's glass roof below her, reflecting the moonlight. Beyond the seashell paths, Eden could see the ocean on the dark horizon.

Eden wasn't dreaming. She had crossed over into the spirit world of Everdark. How long could a living girl exist in such a place? Her stomach rumbled with hunger and tears formed in her eyes. But then she blinked back her sadness and sniffed sharply. She wasn't going to cry anymore. Tears wouldn't save her.

She grunted as she tried to open the windows, but they wouldn't budge. As she searched for something heavy to smash the glass with, the bedroom door opened. The little girl reappeared, sneaking back into the room with a secretive smile.

"What time is it?" Eden asked.

"Still early," Netty said. "Night coming."

"I thought it was already night. The moon is out."

"We don't have no sun," Netty replied sadly.

The little girl moved closer, her eyes glowing against her shimmering indigo skin. Goose bumps spread on the back of Eden's neck.

"Grace went to see Mother Mary," the little girl said.

"Will you get in trouble for being here?"

"Mother Mary call me her favorite," Netty answered proudly. "When you was sleep, I touched your hand. Sure was warm. Like hot bread. Can I touch it again?"

When Eden flinched and moved away, Netty's face crumpled. "You scared of me because I ain't bright."

Eden's heart softened for a moment. Netty was dead and frightening, but she was also a little girl who seemed sad and lonely.

"It—it's not that," she stuttered. "I just don't belong here. Grace even thinks so."

"She don't care about nobody." Netty pouted. "She only want *him*."

Eden forced herself to move closer to Netty. The little girl had started to sniffle, and she leaned down to Netty's height. "Grace doesn't seem to care about anybody but herself."

Netty smirked. "That much true."

"Do . . . do you remember me?" Eden asked.

The little girl frowned as if confused, and then she shook her head. Disappointment flooded Eden's heart.

"Are you sure?" Eden whispered. "In my dream I thought—"

Netty interrupted her. "When Mother Mary brung you here, she say you gon' be our new sister."

Eden's stomach lurched at the words. "Is she keeping you here against your will?"

"No," Netty said. "Mother Mary save me."

"How old are you?"

"Don't remember," she answered.

"That's okay," Eden said. "I'm thinking you're probably at least seven, maybe eight."

Netty shrugged as if the number meant nothing to her. With a trembling hand, Eden slowly reached out and touched Netty's arm. It was ice cold but solid.

Grace entered the room, and Eden jerked her hand away from Netty. The older girl frowned at both of them.

"We need to get her ready for supper," the older girl said.

CHAPTER THIRTEEN

Party Dress

Grace opened the wardrobe to reveal dresses of different hues. The girls argued about which one to choose, but they finally presented Eden with an ivory dress draped over a satin padded hanger.

"What happened to my clothes?" Eden asked.

"They was a disgrace. Mother Mary burned them in the fireplace." Grace pushed the dress into Eden's chest. "Put this on so I can do your hair."

Her faced burned. Eden didn't want to undress in front of these dead girls. But then Grace pointed toward a dressing screen painted with exotic birds.

Eden found a bureau with underclothes that smelled of lavender. She pulled off the nightgown and checked herself for bruises. Eden remembered the witch's long black nails piercing her skin. But her arm was unmarked.

She examined the ivory dress. It was finely made, with puffed sleeves. A very careful hand had stitched seed pearls to the wide collar. She had seen dresses like these on the internet worn by daughters of tycoons and royalty. Girls who lived in mansions and castles. Girls from another time. Eden put on the dress, and it fit her perfectly.

"You done?" Grace's grumpy voice traveled over the dressing screen.

When Eden revealed herself, Netty widened her eyes. "Pretty."

Grace guided her in front of the vanity, and Eden tentatively sat in the silk-covered chair, staring at the older girl in the gilded mirror. Grace gave her another frown but then focused on Eden's hair. She combed out tangles, and Eden winced as the older girl's dead, cold fingers touched her scalp.

"How you get hair like that?" Netty asked.

Eden didn't answer the little girl. Her mother had tight coils that could lengthen with the heat of a flat iron, but Eden had inherited her loose curls from her father.

Grace styled Eden's hair in a high bun with tendrils framing her face. Netty opened the vanity drawer to reveal pearl necklaces and rings with gems of every shade. Blue velvet held other pieces of fine jewelry. Netty placed a strand of pearls around her neck, and Grace chose silver earrings in the shape of tiny, delicate leaves and a sapphire bracelet.

After they finished adorning Eden with accessories, Netty gave her socks with lace frills and patent leather shoes with silver buckles.

"Where does all this come from?" Eden asked.

"Mother Mary," Grace said. "She make it so."

"Before I come here, I ain't never seen clothes like this," Netty said.

"You was dead already," Grace reminded her. "These clothes come after your time."

"You was dead too." The little girl pouted.

Grace steered Eden to a full-length mirror beside the wardrobe. In the reflection, she saw three girls dressed for an extravagant party.

The older girl revealed a rare smile. "Now you ready for supper."

Eden followed the girls down the hallway to a spiral staircase. On the first floor, elaborate crown moldings decorated columns and ceilings. Electric lamps gave a low buzz and emitted a warm glow on the thick patterned rugs.

They traveled through a vast library with tall mahogany shelves built into curved walls. Eden glanced at leather-bound books with gold-lettered spines. Grace then led them into a great room with a heavy-beamed ceiling, and Eden felt a vague tug of memory. She gazed at the glass entry doors. They were the same ones she had peeked into yesterday while on Uncle Willie's tour of the Renata Mansion.

The fireplace filled the great room with warm light, and wood crackled in the hearth. An oil painting hung over the mantel. The frame was covered with a black veil. As Eden looked closer, she realized underneath the gauzy material was the decaying face of a white woman who held a bony smile. Eden shivered as Netty grabbed her hand.

They arrived in the dining room, which had pale blue walls with large glass windows accented with smaller oval ones above each of them. Moonlight glinted off two crystal chandeliers that dangled over a long dining table. At its far end, the witch was seated in a tall chair.

When she rose and sauntered toward them, Eden's heart

raced with distress. The witch looked much different than she had on the moonless beach. She wore a sparkling green dress accented with peacock feathers. Her hair was pressed and coiffed into flowing waves. Beaded crystal necklaces draped around her neck and sparkled in the moonlight. Eden glanced at the witch's nails, but they were covered with black gloves that stopped at her elbows.

"Mother Mary, we did our best to make her presentable," Grace said.

"Ain't she pretty?" Netty suggested.

"She look lovely," the witch answered. "So pleased you joining us for supper, Eden. Come sit down."

Grace and Netty sat at the dining table, but Eden didn't move. Her eyes darted to the dining room entrance.

What if I ran? she thought. *Could I make it to the front doors?*

Sweat beaded on Eden's forehead, and her pearl collar itched. She slowly retreated, tensing her muscles to bolt. But when she turned to run, she bumped into a man dressed in a white servant jacket and screamed.

The man had deep-indigo skin, but there was something wrong with his eyes. Eden stumbled away until she hit the dining table with a painful thud to her leg. When the man moved from the shadows, Eden realized his eyes were covered with pennies.

"Bull, you done gave that girl a mighty fright," the witch said.

The penny-eyed man remained silent as he staggered to the witch's side.

"Usually he wait for the bell," Grace complained.

"He know tonight different," the witch said. "Eden, sit down, so Bull can serve supper."

Eden still thought about running. Maybe if she was fast enough, she could make it to the front doors. The moon hadn't set yet. There was still enough light to find her way back to the woods.

But what if she didn't make it to the doors? What would the witch do after her failed escape? Eden's stomach gave another solution with a loud grumble. She decided that she could try to escape after supper.

When Eden sat next to Netty, the witch turned to her servant. "Old Bull was known for his way around a party in the Big House. Not as a guest, of course. How long you serve them white folks, Bull?"

"I reckon I done forgot, Miss Mary," he answered, his voice raspy, as if unused.

"No matter." The witch took one of Bull's elderly hands into her gloved one. "You serve me now. *Always.*"

Bull bowed his head. "Pleasure all mine, Miss Mary."

"Well, don't keep us waiting!" the witch laughed. "Send supper out."

Bull raised his head and looked directly at Eden. His eerie eyes glowed in the chandelier's light, making the hairs on her arm rise.

As the servant left, the witch turned to Eden. "Don't mind Old Bull's eyes. Got them pennies when they put him down in Orleans cemetery. That's where I found him, you see."

When Bull returned, he brought a platter of cucumber sandwiches and shrimp cocktail in crystal bowls. Netty grabbed one of the sandwiches and plopped it quickly into her mouth. Grace slowly tore the tail off a shrimp before taking a deep bite.

This food was much different from what Eden had eaten at the Gardener family celebration.

"You don't like the appetizers?" the witch asked Eden. "You can wait for the main course."

The girls finished eating, and Bull cleared the plates. Next, he arrived with a rolling service cart with trays of covered food. He placed one tray in front of each of them, and Eden's mouth watered at the savory scents that wafted from underneath the silver domes.

When Bull uncovered her plate, Eden's eyes widened at beef tips covered in heavy gravy, new potatoes drenched in butter, and asparagus spears with shaved parmesan.

The witch gave Eden a cruel smile, making her heart skip, but when her stomach growled again, she quickly picked up her fork for a taste. As she swallowed, she immediately gagged and spit out ash.

Grace snickered into her napkin, and Netty let out a horrified cry. Shocked silent, Eden stared down at the black splotches scattered across her plate.

She grabbed the crystal goblet in front of her. But when the water passed through her lips, her stomach cramped in revulsion as bile threatened to rise up her throat.

The witch tilted her head. "Nourishment only for the dead here."

Eden winced as her insides churned in disgust. Without food or clean water, she wouldn't survive long in this world. Eden pushed her plate away.

"I'm not hungry," she lied.

CHAPTER FOURTEEN

A Stolen Life

For dessert, Bull brought caramel tea rolls, and the Everdark spirits devoured them with ice cream. The witch gave Eden cruel smiles between small bites of food.

When the spirits finished their dessert, the witch rang a small bell for Bull to claim the dishes. "Shall we adjourn?"

"Yes, Mother Mary," Grace and Netty responded in unison.

The girls stood up from the dining table, but Eden remained seated. "Where are we going?" she asked Netty.

"Upstairs to the ballroom," the little girl whispered.

Eden slowly rose from her chair and followed them out of the dining room. Bull passed them on the way, his slow steps guiding him toward the kitchen in the south wing of the mansion.

The witch directed them through the great room, and Eden averted her eyes from the painting of the decaying white woman. Instead, she trained her eyes on the front doors.

Netty grabbed her hand. "Stay close to me."

Eden let the little girl guide her, studying the layout of the mansion for avenues of escape.

They walked into a regal sitting room, where a large mural of palmettos and birds adorned the wall. Fragrant gardenias in a silver vase rested on the fireplace mantel in front of an emerald-cut mirror. The witch opened a door to a flight of stairs, and they went up to a second-floor hallway. On one side, two arched alcoves overlooked the sitting room below, but Eden leaned over the wrought-iron railing on the other side, which opened to the solarium. The glass walls revealed a darkening sky dotted with early stars, and the pool glimmered in the waning moonlight like a gloomy lake.

"Don't like that room," Netty said. "Ain't never learn to swim."

"Does it matter?" Eden asked. "Can you even drown?"

Netty grimaced as if fighting a bad memory. "I stay away from that water."

What happened to you? Eden wondered. *How did you die?*

"No lollygagging." Grace's voice filtered down the hallway ahead of them. "Keep moving."

Eden followed the spirits up another flight of stairs to the third level of the mansion. The grand ballroom showcased a gleaming waxed floor, and wallpaper patterned with garnet hexagons adorned the walls. Black-linen-covered tables with brass candlestick centerpieces were clustered at the rear of the large room. Eden shivered as her breath puffed out small clouds into the freezing air.

The witch disappeared into a cloakroom and emerged dressed in a floor-length sable fur. She held three more coats in her arms. She gave Eden a luxurious fox fur, and Eden reluctantly took it. The coat fit her perfectly and enveloped her in instant warmth.

Netty and Grace put on their furs, and Eden joined them at one of the tables. In front of the ballroom was a film projector and a large screen.

"We ready?" the witch asked.

Netty clapped her hands in glee, her ermine fur wrapped tight under her chin. Grace slumped in her chair, nonchalant in her black mink.

"We gon' watch *Baby Take a Bow*," Netty told Eden.

"Silly child movie," Grace grumbled.

"My movie happy. Ain't sad like yours. Tired of crying," Netty said.

"You need to stop playacting," the older girl snapped. "You ain't a child no more."

The witch approached the table. "Grace, fix your tone. We done talked about this. We can't watch *Imitation of Life* every night. Even I tire of that tragic bright girl. Tonight we watching Netty's movie. Only fair."

"I choose Shirley Temple!" Netty laughed.

Eden sat stiff at the table. Is this what it was like in Everdark? The dead dressed for supper and then watched movies? On its surface, this world didn't seem dangerous. It was extravagant, full of party dresses and priceless jewelry. But Eden remembered the moonless beach, and the witch's long dark nails piercing into her skin. The memory alone made her shiver with dread.

Eden knew this spirit world wasn't safe.

The witch dimmed the lights and then turned on the film projector. A mechanical whir filled the ballroom, and the movie began to play. Netty narrated Shirley Temple's lines from memory, while Grace stared into space. The older girl's mind was elsewhere, far away from the happenings of the ballroom.

When the movie ended and the credits rolled, Eden saw that *Baby Take a Bow* had been made in 1934.

The witch flipped on the lights, and the room grew warmer. The girls shed their coats, but Eden kept the fox fur wrapped tight around her like a protective shield.

"Y'all can leave," the witch said. "I'll escort Eden."

Netty gave Eden a frightened look, but Grace grabbed the little girl by the shoulders and led her out of the ballroom. Eden felt cold and clammy in her coat despite the humid air.

The witch sat at the table. "Do you know how much nerve you got to have to bring furs to an island? Renata Spelling had no common sense, I tell you straight. No matter, I make it cold enough up here to wear these furs now."

Eden shifted in her seat, the fox fur sticking to the sweat that had formed on her neck.

"You like the movie?" the witch asked. "Netty think the world of Shirley Temple, but I know that little white girl probably dead now."

Eden yearned to take the fur off, but she didn't move. She didn't know what the witch was planning for her.

"In time, you can choose a movie," the witch said.

Eden and Natalie had watched lots of movies during their sleepovers, but she was sure that none of their favorites were here in Everdark. She fought a painful prick of tears as she thought of her best friend. Would she ever see Natalie again?

If she didn't escape, Eden wouldn't be a glass flower but a

dead girl, one who would be lost forever in the spirit world of her mother's birthplace.

She didn't want her father choosing a photograph for her memorial service. She didn't want him weeping alone in the world of the living.

Eden took off the fur. "You know I don't belong here. I want to go back to Willow Hammock."

The witch tilted her head, examining Eden's face as if trying to commit it to memory. "Before I was dead, I wanted a lot of things I never got. My life was stolen. Did you know that? Just took from me. So I know how it feel to want something, bright girl. I know all about wanting things you ain't never gon' get."

"I'm sorry your life was stolen," Eden whispered. "But you shouldn't steal mine."

The witch laughed. "Your life ain't been stolen. You came to *me*."

"I didn't—"

"You crossed over, and I found you." The witch's voice filled the room, echoing off the walls.

"It was a mistake," Eden protested.

The witch rose from her chair. Her green gown shimmered in the low candlelight of the ballroom. Eden gaped as the witch's eyes turned solid black, and the room darkened as if on the brink of a storm.

"You belong to me now." The Witch of Everdark pulled off her gloves to reveal long, sharp nails.

When Eden awakened, she was in the north-wing bedroom still wearing the party dress. The witch had sunk her nails into

Eden's skin and plunged her into darkness. She examined her arms again but didn't find any bruises. Only unmarked brown skin.

She slid off the bed and limped to the door, jiggling the locked crystal knob for several minutes before giving up.

After scanning the room, Eden picked up the silk-covered chair and smiled at its heavy weight. But when she threw it at the bedroom window to smash the glass, the chair bounced away as if repelled by strong magic. Eden quickly swerved and slammed to the floor to avoid getting hit, and then stared in shock at the chair toppled on its side.

She tried to control her breathing, taking deep gulps of air. She didn't want another moment like she'd had in the woods or on the moonless beach, where everything seemed hopeless.

When she returned to the window, the moon had set and the courtyard was dim. Stars and clouds were high in the sky. In the distance, Eden saw a splinter of light. A swaying lantern in the distance.

She always go out at night, Netty had said.

Maybe Eden could find a way to escape while the witch was gone. There had to be a way to get out of this room.

Slight movement caught her attention in the dark courtyard. A familiar figure lurked on the seashell path. Two goldenrod eyes appeared in the gloom. The black cat prowled closer to the mansion, and Eden's heart leaped as her breath fogged up the thick glass.

The black cat's tail twitched as it stared up at her. Hope

stirred in Eden's chest. If she could find a way out of the mansion, she could follow the black cat back to the world of the living.

The black cat sat still watching Eden for several moments, but then it turned its gaze toward the beach, in the direction of the witch's swaying lantern. After a few more moments, it trotted away and disappeared into the eternal night.

CHAPTER FIFTEEN
The Loop

Eden was still a prisoner in the witch's mansion. She had tried everything to escape. The windows and doors were blocked by a conjured trick that she didn't know how to break. The witch's power was strong.

She counted her days by the moonrises in Everdark. On the second moonrise, Grace and Netty had arrived at the north-wing bedroom, and Eden quickly realized that the spirits were on some kind of repeating loop. The girls chose a party dress, selected jewelry, and then styled Eden's hair. Afterward, the spirits escorted her to the grand dining room. Bull presented the same supper of beef tips, potatoes, and asparagus followed by caramel tea rolls and ice cream. Although Eden's stomach growled with hunger, she hadn't touched the food. She only braved small sips of rancid water.

In the icy ballroom, the witch draped Eden in the luxurious fox fur. The movie projector played Grace's choice, *Imitation of Life*. The older girl watched with rapt attention as a Black girl named Peola struggled with acceptance from society. This movie was very different from Netty's choice. *Baby Take a Bow* show-cased Shirley Temple singing happy songs and dancing with her father, but *Imitation of Life* focused on Peola passing as white and disowning her mother. Eden wept along with Netty at the tragic ending, and the witch gave them embroidered handkerchiefs for their tears.

When the girls left the ballroom, Eden hadn't asked if she could return to Willow Hammock, because she knew that the witch would refuse her request. So she remained docile and quiet, and the witch didn't sink her sharp nails into Eden's skin.

The loop of events ended when the witch escorted Eden to the north-wing bedroom. When the moon set behind the trees and stars crowded the sky, the witch had left the mansion with her lantern and disappeared into the night.

The black cat hadn't returned.

Now, in the cold brightness of another moonrise, Eden used the sharp edge of a gold brooch to mark her time in Everdark. She stared at the three deep scratches on the hardwood floor.

I have to find a way out of this mansion, she thought.

By now her father may have given up hope that he would find her. Did Dr. Leopold think Eden had drowned in the ocean, forever lost to him? There would be state and local police on Safina Island searching for her. Maybe even Natalie would know that she was missing. Her best friend would be devastated.

Rising from the floor, Eden went to the adjoining bathroom. She found toiletries in a tightly woven basket underneath the porcelain sink. Fancy soaps in the shape of flowers, thick lotions, and scented oils. She drew hot water for the clawfoot tub, then added pink bath salt and watched the crystals foam on the surface. After a few moments, Eden took off her nightgown and sank her body deep into the fragrant water, as curls of steam fogged the hanging mirrors and porcelain tiles.

When the water in the tub grew tepid, Eden dried off with a thick towel that smelled of eucalyptus and blotted her curls dry.

A dark spot on the ceiling caught her attention. Eden stared as rot sprawled down the walls and festered in the grout of the bathroom tiles in a rapid decay. But when she blinked, the mirage disappeared and the room was clean again. Eden slowly moved out of the bathroom, shutting the door.

In the bedroom, she investigated every window and wall but found none of the dark rot. Confused, Eden slid her fingertips over the unblemished surfaces. Was her mind playing tricks on her?

She opened the wardrobe and found a blue day dress with mother-of-pearl buttons. Behind the dressing screen, she gasped when she found a fresh purple bruise on her arm. It hadn't been there when she had soaked in the tub. Eden winced as she touched the delicate skin just above her elbow. This injury hadn't been caused by the witch's nails. She twisted her arm in the moonlight, and the discoloration shimmered like the skin of an Everdark spirit.

Eden put on the day dress with trembling hands, the long sleeves covering up what she had seen. She sat on the bed and willed herself not to cry. She had now seen three moonrises in Everdark, and time was running out. The growls in her stomach had now been replaced with a deep fear.

Eden jumped at the sharp knock at the door, but then Netty poked her head into the room with a wide grin.

"You 'wake?" she asked.

The little girl was wearing a similar day dress but with pink pinstripes. The outfit reminded Eden of old-fashioned candy stripers, the hospital volunteers who assisted doctors and nurses with patient care.

"Brought you something." Netty presented Eden with an orange. "Bull told me to give it to you."

"Thank you." Eden took the fruit.

"Mother Mary downstairs," the little girl said. "She wanna speak with you."

"Do you know what she wants?"

Netty shook her head. "She don't tell me nothing."

Eden stared at the little girl's indigo skin and the way it shimmered in the moonlight like the bruise on her arm. She averted her eyes and put the orange on the nightstand. "We can go now. I'm ready."

Netty escorted Eden down the spiral staircase through the library. They walked across the great room, but Netty signaled for Eden to stop. The door was cracked open, and the voices of Grace and the witch seeped out of the sitting room.

"I done told you, girl. He can't be raised."

"But you promised me!" the older girl pleaded.

"I said I would try," the witch responded. "I ain't never promise."

Netty frowned in disapproval. Eden wondered if this conversation was a part of the repeating loop or if this was something new that was veering the spirits off course.

Eden leaned close to Netty. "Who are they talking about?"

"Almond," she whispered. "The boy Grace love."

She remembered her first night in Everdark, when Netty had agreed Grace didn't like anyone. *She only want him*, the little girl had said.

Eden eased closer to the door, but Netty tugged on her day dress. "Ain't nice to listen to other folks business," she warned.

But Eden didn't need to eavesdrop, because the witch's voice suddenly rose in loud waves, slipping into the great room.

"I don't think he wanna be raised, and what you done told me about that boy ain't got the mettle to conjure him against his will. I can't do nothing with scraps."

"Ain't my love enough?" Grace cried.

Eden widened her eyes at the pain in the older girl's voice. The tone was full of longing and regret, a heavy burden, like the block of ice on her own chest. She didn't know Almond, the boy Grace loved, but she knew that cracked lilt. It was the sound of grief.

When the door flew open, Netty and Eden stumbled several steps away. The older girl frowned, narrowing her eyes at them.

"Is Netty out there?" the witch asked.

"She brung that bright girl," Grace sneered.

"Let them in. We done," the witch said.

Grace moved aside to let them enter the room. Eden could almost feel the chill of the older girl's annoyance as they passed. Grace gave the witch another long look before leaving the room.

The witch was in a chair near the fireplace, where moonlight glinted off the mantel mirror. The gardenia blooms were fragrant in the silver vase, and Eden stared at them longingly.

The center table showcased an extravagant tea set and sliced oranges on a silver platter.

Like Grace and Netty, the witch wore a simple day dress. Her hair was in a thick braid that sloped down her back. She held a teacup, and her long black nails clicked against the porcelain. The witch took a long sip.

"Did you sleep well?" she finally asked.

"No," Eden answered truthfully.

"In time you will." The witch poured more tea into her cup. "Like a baby full of milk."

Netty skipped across the room to a white couch filled with dolls made of sweetgrass, yarn, and fabric. The little girl murmured happy greetings to them. Eden sat stiffly on the edge of a wingback chair.

The witch beamed at Netty. "One of the joys since I come here is seeing that child thrive."

The little girl smiled at the witch and organized her dolls in a tight circle. She was happy and content. Not grumpy and sad, like Grace.

"When I found Netty, she was up high in one of them great oaks. Her mama had flew off, you see. Poor child thought water still covered the land. Last big hurricane was in 1809, when them Spellings claimed they owned us." The witch laughed, as if a bold lie had been told. She took another long sip of tea before she continued. "Over a hundred years had passed by the time I seen Netty in that tree. She the first one I found when I come here. Reckon she still be up in that tree if it weren't for me."

Netty's delighted hums filled the room. The witch stared at Eden as if waiting for a response.

"Maybe she was waiting for her mom to come back and get her," Eden finally said.

The witch huffed in disagreement. "Once they fly away, they don't never come back. For nobody."

Netty had told Eden that the witch had saved her. Maybe it was true that the little girl wasn't being held against her will after all.

Eden squirmed in her chair. "When can I go home?"

The witch tilted her head in confusion. "You *are* home."

Eden moved her hand over her hidden bruise. Did the witch already know that she was changing? Was it already too late for her? Eden let out a shaky breath.

"Bright girls don't come here because they happy," the witch said. "When I found you on my beach, I seen the sadness in you. Somebody leave you, too? Was it your mama?"

Eden had been drawn to Everdark because of her deep grief. The darkness and danger had felt like a comfort. Her lips trembled, and she fought the prick of tears, but they fell down her cheeks.

"No need to be shame about crying," the witch said softly. "No matter if your mama leave you. You my daughter now. Everything gon' be fine."

A rush of anger spread through Eden. The witch had captured her on the beach like prey. She knew keeping Eden as a prisoner in this spirit world would result in her death.

"I'm not your daughter," Eden said, a defiant boom in her voice.

Netty stopped playing with her dolls and stared at Eden with concerned, glowing eyes. The witch took another sip of tea, and her quiet wrath filled the room like a storm brewing above the moonless beach.

"I see we won't be having a cordial talk. Lack of sleep done made you ornery," the witch finally said. "Netty, take this bright girl up to her room so she can rest for supper."

The little girl took Eden by the arm, her cold touch now familiar. After Netty closed the door to the sitting room, she frowned. "You don't need to be making Mother Mary cross with you. Ain't smart."

Eden didn't respond because Netty didn't understand. The witch had found her when she was a lost, confused spirit. She hadn't been a living girl.

"Is it true?" Netty's voice softened. "You ain't got no mama no more?"

Eden couldn't speak, fearing the words would spiral her deeper into grief. When she nodded, Netty moved closer.

"You just like me," she whispered. "I ain't got no mama neither."

CHAPTER SIXTEEN
Dead Longer Than Alive

Eden followed Netty back into the great room. She glanced at the heavy wood beams before settling her eyes on the oil painting above the fireplace mantel. In the moonlight, the dark veil couldn't hide what was underneath. The woman's features had once been beautiful, but now the brown curls framed a face that was rotting. Pale skin sloped off, revealing bone and gristle.

Eden moved closer to the fireplace and stared at the painting. "Who's that woman?" she asked.

"Renata Spelling," Netty answered.

Charles Spelling's wife, Eden thought. *The one who cursed him to death.*

"Why does she look like that?"

"Don't worry about her none," Netty said.

Eden scanned the room with a new focus. Silver light filtered through the glass front doors, scattering tiny prisms on the floor. She moved toward them, but the little girl grabbed her hand in a cold grip.

"Stay close to me." Netty's luminous eyes held a warning.

Eden retreated and lingered on the details of her surroundings. Delicate crystal figurines were on a long table behind the leather couch. Stuffed birds and hunting game decorated the walls. She also noticed several closed doors, and her mind plotted. Maybe the doors led to possible avenues for escape?

"Where's your room, Netty?" Eden picked up a crystal owl, surprised at its weight.

Netty took the figurine away from Eden, returning it to the long table. "My room above the kitchen in the south wing."

"Do you ever leave the mansion?" Eden asked carefully.

The little girl glanced at the closed door to the sitting room. "I keep Mother Mary company and play with my dolls. Ain't had none before I was dead."

"I'm sorry," Eden said.

"Never mind your sorry," Netty said. "Best be getting you upstairs now."

Eden followed Netty into the library, with its mahogany curved walls and faint smell of paper. She perused the bookcases full of leather-bound volumes. These shelves provided a lifetime of reading. Eden wondered if anyone had read these books or if the spines remained uncracked, the pages untouched.

Her curiosity deflated when she returned to the north-wing bedroom, because there was nothing left for her to discover in this space.

Netty sat in the silk-covered chair. "I can keep you company if you like."

She studied the little girl for a few moments. Kind and sweet, Netty tugged at Eden's heartstrings. "Guess I was wrong about your age."

"That much true. Been dead longer than alive," Netty answered.

Eden sat at the foot of the bed, her day dress spilling around her. She fiddled with the mother-of-pearl buttons. "Do you remember when you were . . . before you came here?"

"Don't dwell on Spelling time," Netty answered quickly.

Eden swallowed. If the witch was telling the truth, Netty had been enslaved when she was alive. She had died while the Spelling Plantation's tabby walls survived the 1809 hurricane. Maybe it was good that Netty didn't linger on those memories. Eden knew enslavement didn't have varying degrees of treatment. There weren't any acts of kindness or compassion that diminished the brutal reality. On Safina Island, her ancestors had been treated as chattel, the highest form of oppression.

"You told me once you didn't like water. Is it because of the hurricane?" Eden asked.

Netty looked away, and Eden's cheeks burned with regret. She was being rude to this spirit, asking about the details of her death.

"I shouldn't have asked you something like that. I'm sorry."

"Stop saying sorry." Netty's voice was sharp, edged with irritation. "That word ain't got no meaning here."

Eden remained quiet. Maybe in Everdark, the dead had no need for regrets. Several moments passed, and then the little girl crossed her arms against her chest as if she were cold.

"I remember what I seen in the water," Netty whispered. "Ain't never gon' forget what was in them waves."

Eden knew hurricanes overwhelmed the land. The combination of wind and water had a devastating effect. Many animals and people perished. She shuddered when she thought about what had been in the water beneath Netty's tree.

"What did Mother Mary mean when she said your mom flew away? Did . . . did she turn into an angel?"

"My mama weren't no angel. She flew back home with the magic she brung with her from across the water. When the hurricane come through Safina, she got hold of some good wind and took off, but she ain't take me."

Eden didn't know what to say. The witch stated that once a spirit flew away, they didn't come back. For anyone.

"I'm sor—" Eden stopped herself. "Maybe she had her reasons for leaving."

Netty gave her a sad smile. "How your mama leave you?"

Several fat teardrops slid down Eden's cheeks, dampening her dress. Netty approached and hugged her, the little girl's coldness a reprieve from the hot sobs of Eden's grief.

The memories of her mother's sudden death still took Eden's breath away. The stricken look on her father's face when he came to pick her up from school. Natalie's tight hug as she wailed. The sharp pain, like a dagger to her heart.

"It was her brain . . . the doctor said it was an aneurysm." She paused, swallowing the cold medical term for the blood vessel that had ruptured and taken her mother's life. "She thought it was a bad headache. We didn't get a chance to say goodbye."

Eden wiped her face as Netty pulled a quilt from the wardrobe. As she wrapped her in the quilt's warmth, the gesture reminded Eden of her best friend. In the world of the living, Natalie had given comfort. Now in Everdark, Netty was keeping the wolves of grief away.

"Sometime we don't get a say on how folks leave us," the little girl said.

Eden burrowed deeper into the quilt. "I'm tired of being trapped in this house."

She held her breath and waited as the words hung in the air, and the heavy silence between them lingered for a few seconds.

Netty brushed loose curls from Eden's face. "Mother Mary like to picnic on the beach. Let me see what I can do."

Eden exhaled in relief. "Thank you."

After Netty left the north-wing bedroom, Eden stared at the orange on the nightstand, a tiny sun in the moonlight. She still wasn't sure if she could trust the Everdark spirit, because there was something the little girl wasn't sharing with her. But if Eden could get outside and away from the mansion, there was a chance she could escape and find her way back to Willow Hammock.

Eden grabbed the orange, peeling its skin away. It was a gift from the witch's servant. Maybe this was something she could eat. She hesitated before taking a deep bite. Tart juice didn't fill her mouth, only the bitterness of ash. Spitting out the pulp, she threw the orange across the room.

She hated herself for having hope, for believing things would be different. Eden's fresh bruise pulsed with her heartbeat, and she pulled the quilt tighter around her. In the bright moonlight, lines of dark rot fractured the ceiling. But this time when she blinked, the decay didn't disappear.

CHAPTER SEVENTEEN
A Fallen Star

As Grace and Netty prepared Eden for supper, she didn't care about the beautiful party dress. She was indifferent to the double-strand pearl necklace and amethyst earrings. Eden stared into the vanity mirror and only saw a bright girl whose fate was doomed.

Behind the dressing screen, she had examined her arm again before she put on the lavender party dress. The bruise on her arm had sprawled to her wrist, and cold dread spread down her spine.

When Bull placed the tray of food in front of her, Eden didn't crave a taste of the savory meat or buttered herbs on her tongue. She didn't yearn to crunch the fresh asparagus between her teeth. She no longer cared about her hunger, only her impending death.

In the icy ballroom the projector played the witch's choice, *Top Hat*. Eden had never seen the movie, but she recognized Fred Astaire and Ginger Rogers as the famous dancing duo. The witch sang the song "Cheek to Cheek" and performed the choreography with precision. Netty clapped in full glee, while Grace politely praised with weak claps.

It was the first time Eden had seen the witch joyful. She was a natural talent, with a lovely voice that caressed the walls, and the blue sequined dress she wore sparkled with her graceful moves.

When the movie was over and the girls had left, the witch continued to waltz around the ballroom as if she were dancing with Fred Astaire himself. When she finally twirled back to the table, her starry indigo face was flushed with happiness.

"Remind me of my time on the stage," she said in a wistful voice. "I miss them lights on my skin. That rumble of nerves in my stomach before the curtain rose up for showtime."

Eden raised her eyebrows in surprise, and the witch chuckled. Her satin-gloved hand trailed down her neck as she pondered a memory.

"Shoulda been on Broadway dazzling them white folks," the witch said with reverence.

"You were a performer?" Eden asked.

"Thought I was a simple island girl?" the witch snapped. "Some saltwater who ain't never been nowhere?"

The room dimmed and flickered with the witch's change of mood, and Eden knew that she should tread carefully. She almost apologized but kept the word hidden under her tongue. Netty would have been proud.

"You're a very good dancer and singer," she said. "Broadway would have been honored to have you."

The witch beamed at the compliment as she took off her sable coat. Eden mirrored the action and did the same with the fox fur. The faraway look had returned to the witch's face as she pondered her life.

"When them stocks crashed in 'twenty-nine, white men was

jumping out of windows, and I had to come back to Safina." The witch's eyes glowed in anger. "All of us was lost during that time. But unlike them white men, my color gave me no protection, and being a woman didn't help me none neither."

The witch's face twitched at the injustice of her life. "Charles and Renata Spelling used to come up to Harlem and watch me perform. They knew what I could do. I was the headliner everybody wanted to see. Weren't nothing for them to stay after a show and have a drink with me. Bonded fast because we was Southern folks in the city. We had left Safina for the bigger world. But when the hard times come, Renata Spelling acted like she was doing a favor letting me wash and clean for her. Treated me like I was nothing."

The witch sprang up from the table and paced the ballroom floor, the low candlelight wavering with her agitation. Eden shifted in her chair as the witch continued her rant.

"Life pulled a big trick on me." She laughed bitterly. "No matter, I pull the tricks now."

After her anger quelled, the witch returned to the table with a quiet reserve. The beautiful woman had been cheated in her life, Eden realized. Who knew what the witch could have been in a different time under different circumstances? With her talent, she could have easily been on any stage in the world that she wanted. A renowned singer and dancer on Broadway or a famous actress in Hollywood. Eden had seen the proof with her own eyes. The world had only seen her as a simple saltwater girl who could only be a maid. Now in death, she was a bitter spirit, a fallen star.

Eden shivered in the ballroom as the witch wrestled with her haunted memories. She finally reached out and touched Eden's arm, the gloved hand resting over the bruise hidden under the sleeve of Eden's party dress.

"Can feel the bright leaking from you," the witch said softly. "Won't be long, daughter."

Eden tensed at the words, but she knew they were true. If she couldn't find her way back to Willow Hammock and the world of the living, she would be dead soon. The proof was on her skin. A burst of anxiety spun around in her stomach.

Did the witch know that Eden's brown skin was turning the shade of eternal night? All she had to do was pull up her sleeve to reveal the gruesome metamorphosis. But Eden slowly moved away from the witch's grasp.

"Please let me go," she whispered.

"No need for you to go back now," the witch stated. "This where you belong."

Eden had the urge to get on her knees and plead to the witch. But she knew that it wouldn't make a difference. She saw the conviction in the strong lift of the witch's chin. Begging wouldn't change her mind. Eden wasn't full of magic, but the witch had still claimed her. She was taking Eden's life to satisfy the longing for another eternal daughter.

"I'll never belong here," Eden said as a wave of hatred spread over her, cold and bitter. "Even if you let me die here, it still won't make me your daughter."

The witch took off her gloves, revealing long dark nails in the ballroom's candlelight. "Gardeners always think they better than everybody else because of all that land. But y'all ain't the only ones who come across the water with magic."

With the snap of her finger, all the candles blew out in the ballroom. Wisps of gray smoke wavered around Eden. Starlight filtered through the windows, and the witch's eyes glowed in the darkness.

"This ain't Safina. Everything here belong to *me*." The witch's voice was now laced with indignation. "You don't own nothing here. The sooner you learn that, the better. Now get up."

Eden slowly rose from her chair, her body trembling. Her hatred had quickly turned back to fear. The witch gave Eden a cruel smile as she caressed her cheek like a cherished doll.

"Shall we adjourn?" she asked.

They left the ballroom, and the witch hummed the melody of "Cheek to Cheek" as they traveled through the mansion. The witch escorted her to the north-wing bedroom, sharp nails wrapped tight around Eden's arm in an unspoken warning. When the door closed and Eden jiggled the crystal knob, she gasped at her hand. The indigo bruise had now spread from her wrist to her fingertips, the skin shimmering like a constellation of stars.

CHAPTER EIGHTEEN

Whispers in the Dark

Eden changed into her nightgown and burrowed under a quilt. She stared at the cracks of rot on the ceiling. There were more of them now, expanding like tiny rivers on a map.

Although the bruise had spread on her right arm, the rest of her body remained unmarked and brown. But Eden knew that this was only the beginning. If she stayed in Everdark, more bruises would appear, and they would spread on her skin like the rivulets of rot on the ceiling.

A scratching sound caught Eden's attention, and she cocked her head, trying to identify the source. The noise reminded her of small claws. Did Everdark have rats? She focused on the sound. No, not the scurrying of rodents. This noise had a pattern.

Eden crept out of bed and edged closer to one of the walls, pressing her ear against its surface. The scratching had stopped, but then the bedroom door opened with a low creak.

She waited for a moment, a quick breath. "Netty?"

When no one answered, Eden padded quietly across the floor. Standing inches from the cracked door, she called out the little girl's name again. Her fingers trembled with fear, but she jerked the door open only to find the hallway empty.

Despite endless hours of trying, Eden had failed to find a way out of the north-wing bedroom, and now the door had opened of its own volition. Was this a trap the witch had set for her? Eden didn't care. The opportunity for escape was too much for her to ignore. She would take her chances.

Eden slipped down the hallway to the spiral staircase. Leaning over the curved banister, she saw no one at the bottom. Her heart thumped in her chest as she crept into the library, slinking into the shadows.

Someone was in the room.

Bull stood in front of a bookcase. In the dappled light of the library lamps, his copper-lidded eyes glinted. Instead of a white servant jacket, he wore dress slacks and a sweater vest over a starched shirt. He reminded Eden of her father, a distinguished man of letters.

No longer shuffling, Bull walked in a confident gait along the shelves, inspecting volumes. He looked decades younger, his indigo skin smooth and unlined. After much consideration, Bull chose two books and placed them under his arm. His soft whistles followed him out of the room.

Eden waited several minutes before darting through the library to the great room. Bull was nowhere to be seen. The fireplace crackled in the hearth, emitting a bright orange glow. Eden examined the oil painting above the mantel and frowned. The black veil had been lifted, revealing a gaping ripped hole. The decaying woman was missing.

A panic pulsed down her bruised arm. Renata Spelling must be lurking in the mansion. Eden quickly searched the great room but found that she was alone; the ticking of the grandfather clock was the only sound.

Eden's fears of the ruined spirit were soon forgotten when she focused on the front doors. It was night in Everdark, and she knew that she could get lost without the moon to guide her back to the woods, but she wasn't going to waste this opportunity.

She rushed in a full sprint toward the glass doors, but a blunt force pushed her away. Eden's body went airborne, and she fell hard on her backside. Stunned and sore, she got up and adjusted her nightgown.

On the floor, a line of dried flowers sprinkled with red powder was scattered in a jagged line. She hadn't seen it in the low light. Eden bent down for a closer look. When she touched the mysterious mix of powder and flowers, an electric shock jolted her fingers. She sprang back and yelped. Static twisted in Eden's hair, making it rise from her neck. The front doors of the mansion were protected with the witch's conjured magic.

Eden flattened her curls with shaky hands and started toward the sitting room, but another open door caught her attention. Keeping a wide berth from the jagged line of powder and flowers, Eden discovered a flight of stairs leading down into darkness.

She didn't know what could be lurking down there. The ruined spirit of Renata Spelling could be waiting for her. But it could also lead out of the mansion.

Taking a deep breath of courage, Eden slowly descended the stairs.

* * *

The glow from the great room's fireplace provided weak light as Eden stayed close to the wall. Using her arms and hands as a guide, she stepped carefully until she reached the bottom of the stairs. Damp soil with a musky undertone filled Eden's nose with a familiar scent.

Like in the dream, she remembered.

Eden turned to look back up at the stairs and felt a tugging of memory. She had been here before. Now she realized the dark, hidden place in her dream was the lower level of the witch's mansion.

Instead of a dirt floor, Eden's bare feet stood on cold stone. She peered into an open door to her immediate right. Fumbling along the walls, she found a light switch, and low-hanging bulbs fizzed above her. Eden squinted at murals on the walls. Carnival scenes of clowns and elephants. Dancing acrobats and ferocious tigers. White sheets covered large furniture in the room. Pulling off one of the sheets, Eden coughed as dust drifted in the air. She unveiled a green felt pool table and guessed that she was in some kind of game room.

She peeked back into the long hallway, where several closed doors were on each side. Leaving the game room lights on, she wandered down to the first door but found it locked.

Eden heard a noise behind the second door, a muted shuffling. She pressed her ear against the rough wood and listened. After a few moments, she heard a voice from the other side, a desperate whisper.

Eden jerked away from the door. The whispers grew into a chorus of voices, and a loud thump from another closed door made her cry out in surprise. Frantic chants rose in the damp air. But unlike in the dream, she understood the words of the eager pleas.

"Help us! Please help us!"

Her heart leaped in terror as the floor vibrated beneath her feet and the hallway doors trembled. Eden remembered that in the dream, they had splintered and tumbled open. She didn't want to find out if dark shadows would race out from behind those doors.

Eden fled down the hallway and rushed back up the stairs. Stumbling hard, she fell and scraped her knee. Limping the rest of the way, she distanced herself from whatever dwelled in the lowest level of the mansion.

Strong arms grabbed her by the shoulders at the top of the stairs, and her scream was muffled by a cold hand.

"How you get out your room?" Grace narrowed her eyes at Eden.

She took a gulp of air when the older girl removed her hand. "What's down there?"

"Ain't none of your concern," Grace replied.

The older girl shut the door and pulled Eden into the great room. The barrier of dried flowers still remained on the floor. When Grace left a footprint in the red powder, it had no effect on the spirit. The witch's magic had been conjured only for the living.

Near the fireplace, a shadowed figure stared at them. A white woman wearing a red evening gown. Skin sagged on her face, exposing decaying muscle and bone. She raised a skeletal hand at the girls, as if saying hello. Eden shivered at the greeting.

"Get on from here," Grace hissed.

Renata Spelling turned and sauntered toward the sitting room, her bony fingers dragging against the wall.

Grace grabbed Eden's hand. "Ain't safe for you to be out here."

The older girl guided them through the library, and Eden looked behind her, hoping not to see the ruined spirit following them. Upstairs in the north-wing bedroom, Eden sat on the bed and hid her bruised hand under her thigh when Grace went to the bathroom.

The older girl returned with a warm, wet towel. "Don't go gallivanting in this house at night. Too many things would love to take a bite out of you."

Eden suddenly realized that Renata Spelling had opened the bedroom door. She shuddered as she thought about how the spirit had been probably watching her. Hidden in the shadows, waiting for the right moment to pounce.

"Why is Renata Spelling here in the mansion?" Eden asked.

"What she deserve," the older girl mumbled.

Grace cleaned Eden's scraped knee, pausing to stare at the bright red blood on the towel. After a few moments, she quickly resumed her duty.

Eden winced at the throbbing pain. "I heard whispers behind locked doors. They . . . they were asking for help."

"Ain't no help coming for them," Grace said.

"Who are they?" Eden asked. "Are . . . are they like me?"

"Nobody here bright like you."

Eden let the older girl finish treating her knee. Despite her harsh tone, Grace was gentle with her cold hands.

"Thank you," Eden said.

Grace sat next to her on the bed and slumped her shoulders. "You better be glad Mother Mary ain't here. You more trouble than you worth."

Eden stared at the older girl. She had changed back into her green-striped day dress, her ears and neck bare of any jewelry. Eden wanted to ask Grace about Almond. Why did she need the witch to summon him? Despite her curiosity, Eden kept these questions under her tongue. She remembered Grace's tragic tone from the sitting room. Eden knew that grief carried a heavy burden.

"Did you know Netty from before?" she asked instead.

Grace huffed at her question. "If you asking if I was a slave, answer is no. Them Spellings stayed on the mainland in my time. Weren't no mansion."

"Do you remember . . . your life?"

Grace's face tightened. "Born and raised in Willow Hammock on family land."

Eden inhaled a sharp breath. "Are . . . are you a Gardener?"

"I ain't a Gardener girl," she answered. "I'm a Brown."

Grace didn't share the Gardener physical traits, so it had been a slim chance that she was a relative. Yet Eden was surprised at the disappointment she felt. Maybe some part of her wanted to have a connection to this spirit. Even if it was a distant one. At least she had met some of Grace's relatives in Willow Hammock. She was most likely blood kin to Miss Nadine, Little Betsy, and Miss Melba.

"Where did Mother Mary find you?" Eden asked.

Grace quickly rose from the bed, and the frown returned to the older girl's face. "Stay in this room. No matter if that door open or not."

Eden slowly nodded in agreement, and Grace left the north-wing bedroom. Burrowing back underneath the quilt, she now wondered if the dreams she'd had in her mother's old room had been glimpses of her future. Maybe the dreams had been warnings.

She gently rubbed her bruised arm. How many moonrises did she have left in this spirit world? Eden had failed to find an avenue of escape. She was still trapped in Everdark. But now she knew about the lower level of the mansion and had learned something new.

She wasn't the witch's only prisoner.

CHAPTER NINETEEN
The Solarium

A cold hand shook Eden awake, and she blinked and squinted at the moonlight coming through the windows. Netty stood over the bed. "Happy day!"

Eden pushed up against the pillows. "Does Mother Mary want to talk to me again?"

The little girl grinned widely. "We heading out to the beach for a picnic."

Eden straightened her shoulders. "We're . . . we're going outside?"

"Told you I was gon' see to it." Netty beamed. "Time to get up. Need to pick out clothes."

The little girl was already dressed in a high-necked blouse and long blue skirt with boots that peeked out from underneath. Her hair was no longer pressed straight but plaited up into several sections, some of them defying gravity while others curved around her small neck.

Eden watched as Netty skipped to the wardrobe. Now that she knew how old the girl was, or rather, how long the little girl had been dead, she found Netty's childish movements out of place. Too immature for someone who had dwelled in a place for over two hundred years.

"Have you talked with Grace yet?" Eden asked.

The little girl started to hum as she perused the wardrobe. "Need something to cover them arms and legs."

"Did Grace say anything to you?" Eden asked again. "About what happened last night?"

The little girl stopped humming and approached the bed. The look on her face had changed. Netty's forehead creased with concern, and her luminous eyes turned serious and stern. Then the little girl slowly put her finger to her lips.

"Grace don't like the beach," Netty said in a loud, bright voice. "She ain't coming."

Eden understood the hint the little girl gave her. She wouldn't jeopardize this opportunity. A picnic meant leaving the mansion. Netty returned to the wardrobe to search for appropriate clothes.

"I'll go freshen up while you pick out something for me to wear," she said.

In the bathroom, Eden stared at the walls. The rot had now spread farther. She wondered if Grace had seen the decay. The older girl hadn't mentioned anything last night. Could the spirits even see the rot that festered within the mansion walls?

Eden approached the mirror. Her cheekbones were sunken, her lips thinner. She quickly averted her gaze, not wanting to see her hungry eyes. The porcelain sink was still untouched by the mansion's decay, so she splashed her face and washed off her arms and legs with soap.

Won't be long, daughter, the witch had said.

"I'm leaving this mansion, so we'll see about that." Eden's defiant voice echoed off the blighted bathroom tiles.

Eden grabbed a small towel to hide her bruised skin and returned to the bedroom. Netty had chosen a high-necked blouse with long ruffled sleeves and a long skirt the color of hibiscus tea. Eden disappeared behind the silk dressing screen and put on the clothes. They fit her perfectly, a marvel of the witch's magic.

She stared down at her hand. There was no way she would be able to hide it from Netty any longer. The little girl would see it and know that she was changing.

When Eden came out from behind the dressing screen, she found Netty waiting by the bed with a pair of sturdy boots.

"Got to keep that stubborn sand out," the little girl said.

Eden approached her slowly and offered her hand. Netty stared at the indigo skin and dark nails for a few moments before speaking.

"We gon' need to get you some gloves too," the little girl said.

Eden blinked back tears and nodded. She now understood the little girl's secret language. Netty presented her with gloves and a hat with a long blue ribbon.

They left the north-wing bedroom. As they traveled through the library, Eden tried to see if the books that Bull had taken were still gone, but there were no gaps in the shelves. The volumes were snugged tight, like perfect leather teeth.

In the great room, Eden tensed, but no line of dried flowers or red powder waited for her. No danger of electric shock. Only the dappled light of the moon striped the floor.

Eden turned to the fireplace and looked above the mantel. The black veil now covered the oil painting. Renata Spelling was present in her red gown, with a smile frozen on her face.

Netty pulled her forward to the sitting room, but Eden kept her eyes on the woman in the painting, wondering if the ruined spirit was following her moves, waiting for the next opportunity to catch Eden in her bony hands.

As they walked into the solarium, Eden realized that it was the first time she had entered this room. The moonlight pierced the glass roof and showered everything in pale silver light. The aquamarine tiled pool was surrounded by four pillars on each side, along with vases of big-leaf ferns and blooming begonia. A small fountain gurgled in front of the mermaid statue at the far end of the pool.

Netty veered away to the farthest wall, but Eden moved to the pool's edge. The water wasn't clear like she had expected. Instead, it was the color of an ocean on the brink of a storm. She stared into the brackish water as bubbles appeared at the surface.

Dark figures swam in the pool. Gold-flecked scales sparkled and long eel-like tails jerked from side to side. When Eden saw the glint of sharp teeth, she hastily joined Netty at the far wall.

Soon afterward the witch entered the solarium. She wore similar clothes to Netty and Eden, a high-necked blouse with a long brown skirt and leather boots. Her hair was still in the long, thick braid. She held a pink parasol in her right gloved hand. Bull followed closely behind her. He no longer wore the distinguished clothes of a professor but his servant uniform. Did the witch know that he took books from the library? Was it even allowed? In the moonlight, Bull's face was heavily lined with wrinkles and the pennies glowed amber over his eyes. A sliver of doubt crept into Eden's mind, but she pushed it away. She was certain it had been Bull browsing the shelves last night.

He gave the witch a basket covered with a linen cloth. Eden could smell fresh-baked bread and the tangy zest of oranges. Her stomach lurched at the memory of eating ashy pulp in the north-wing bedroom, and she swallowed slowly to keep the bile down. Eden already knew there was nothing in the basket that she could eat.

The witch walked along the edge of the pool. "Netty told me you don't like being shut in, so I figure if you get some moon on your face then your temperament may improve."

"Netty's right, I don't like being inside all the time," Eden said, using the little girl's secret language. "Thank you, Mother Mary, for listening and taking me to the beach."

The witch smiled warmly at Eden's civility. "You welcome, daughter."

She motioned Netty to come forward, but the little girl stayed near the wall. It wasn't until the witch walked to the mermaid statue away from the pool's edge that the little girl moved forward to take the picnic basket.

Eden started to follow her but turned to look back at Bull. The servant stood with his hands folded in front of him. After locking eyes with Netty for a moment, he nodded and left the room.

The little girl opened the solarium door and skipped out, her laughter bouncing off the solarium glass. She was now safe in the courtyard and away from the pool.

"Shall we adjourn?" the witch extended her hand.

Behind Eden there was a loud splash in the pool, but she didn't dare look back to see what had broken the surface. Instead she stared at the witch's gloved hand, the long black nails hidden underneath.

Heavy, wet footsteps echoed on the tiled floor. Eden held her breath as an amphibian croak echoed in the solarium. She tried her best not to shiver or show fear. After a few tense seconds, she heard a diving splash. Whatever had lurked behind her was now back in the pool's depths.

"You shaking like a leaf, bright girl." The witch smiled, her beauty undeniable in the gilded light. "But glad you ain't turn around to see. Woulda gave you a mighty fright."

CHAPTER TWENTY

The Moonlit Beach

Eden followed the witch out of the solarium, and the moonlight glared into her eyes. The courtyard looked almost the same as it had during Uncle Willie's tour. The seashell paths meandered through plots of low-cut grass and small fountains. Large ceramic jars gleamed under the moon. Flowers clustered in small gardens, their colors amplified by the Everdark sky.

Eden strolled down the pathway, her boots crunching softly on the shells. The ocean appeared before her and waves crashed against the black shore. The briny smell of salt was in the air, mixing with courtyard blossoms and waterlogged driftwood.

Netty pulled a blanket from the picnic basket, spreading it near a sand dune covered with beach grass. Eden removed her hat and stared out at the vastness of the ocean, the horizon a faint midnight line. She sat beside the little girl as the witch opened her parasol and wandered down the beach to meet the waves.

"How you feel now?" Netty asked.

Eden took a deep inhale, the air cool and crisp in her lungs. Despite everything, she did feel better.

"It's nice to be outside," she finally said.

Eden was free of the mansion, but she was still in Everdark. Other than the three of them, the beach was desolate and empty. But farther down, she noticed woods in the distance, and her heart started to race.

The witch roamed along the shore, the waves soaking her long skirt with foam, the parasol hiding her face.

"We can speak free now," Netty said. "How long your arm been like that?"

Eden looked down at her gloved hand. "Started last moonrise. It was spreading, but now it's stopped."

Netty pressed her lips together in worry. "Sign of the blowback."

"What's ... what's a blowback?"

"Laying tricks that ain't yours got a price." The little girl met her eyes. "Mother Mary took from the elder spirits when she brung the mansion here. Sun set and ain't never come back up. She mark our skin too. Real color drain out."

Eden thought of the whispers in the lower levels of the mansion. Grace had told her that they weren't bright like her.

"Last night, Renata Spelling opened my door. I went down to the lower level. I heard people behind locked doors ... they were asking for help. Are those the elder spirits?"

Netty nodded. "Grace told me, but she ain't to be trusted."

The first night Eden had met Grace and Netty, the girls seemed at odds. She had thought it was just a sibling rivalry, but now she realized it was something deeper; some kind of betrayal had happened between them.

The witch made no secret that she had found Netty in an oak tree and Bull in a graveyard, bringing them both to the mansion. She had found Eden on the beach.

"Where did Mother Mary find Grace?" Eden asked. "When I asked her, she wouldn't tell me."

"Mother Mary ain't find her," Netty said. "She come here on her own."

The older girl had sought out the witch. Maybe she came for protection or she thought the witch was powerful enough to raise Almond. Eden knew Grace wouldn't tell her the reason. The older girl kept her motivations hidden.

"Can you see the rot inside the house?" Eden asked.

Netty shook her head. "Sometime I find Mother Mary in a room with a bad look on her face. Make me think she done seen something she don't like. Maybe this why Old Buzzard come here. Reckon he smell the rot in this world."

In the sketchbook, Eden's mother had drawn the god-spirit who took human form to walk the world of the living. The one who waited at the crossroads. Eden shuddered remembering her great-aunt's warning of eternal suffering and pain.

Always a price to pay with his offer, Aunt Susanna had said.

Eden wondered if the witch was seeking the god-spirit. Was she looking for him at the crossroads? Did she want Old Buzzard to stop the blowback of her stolen magic?

"Where does Mother Mary go at night?" Eden asked.

"We out of time," Netty said. "Hush now."

The witch was returning from her beach walk, twirling the parasol. When she approached the blanket, she closed and spiked it deep in the sand.

Lying next to Netty, she sighed. "I remember when them Spellings would spend all day out here."

The witch pulled off her gloves, and Eden stared warily at

the long black nails. Netty snuggled up to the witch, curving into her body like a small spoon. The spirits fluttered their eyes closed like cats on a lazy afternoon.

Since coming to Everdark, Eden had observed and listened. She had also done the math. Netty had perished in the 1809 hurricane and was the oldest spirit by far. Grace said the mansion hadn't been built yet during her lifetime, so she had died sometime before 1926, but Eden couldn't be sure. Bull's year of death was still uncertain, but she felt it was before Grace's birth. Maybe even during Netty's Spelling time. Eden guessed the witch had met her tragic end in the 1930s because of the movies they watched in the ballroom. The same time period as Charles Spelling's cursed death.

"Picnic days was the best days." The witch's voice was soft and low, but her eyes remained closed. "It would be so peaceful in the house. No nagging or fretting."

"Did the Spellings stay at the Renata Mansion all year round?" Eden asked.

Netty's eyes snapped open. "I done told you not to call it that."

Eden swallowed hard. A chill crept up her neck as she wondered how she would be punished, but the witch didn't even open her eyes.

"Don't worry about her none, Netty," she said. "Time will teach her soon enough."

"I know it's your mansion," Eden quickly said. "Everything here is yours."

"That be right. Being dead got perks." The witch's lips curled into a smirk. "Now we be the ones who lay out on the beach and do nothing. Not a Spelling in sight."

Netty gave Eden a warning look before closing her eyes again. She understood the little girl's message to stay quiet.

Eden pulled her knees up to her chest. The waves rolled onto the beach, crests tinged silver from the moon.

She turned and stared at the woods in the distance. It was the way back to Willow Hammock, her father, and relatives. This was her avenue of escape.

Netty and the witch slumbered on the blanket. Their breathing had slowed and deepened. She observed the rise and fall of their chests, the flutter of their dreaming eyelids. Eden counted the breaths of the slumbering spirits. One breath, two breaths. After the hundredth breath, an eternity of waiting, Eden rose from the blanket.

Her heartbeat boomed in her ears, louder than the crash of the waves. She crept backward slowly off the blanket. One step, two steps. Her boots sank into the black sand. Turning toward the woods, Eden tried to measure the distance.

How fast can I run? she wondered.

There were dangerous things that lurked within the mansion. Secrets that could harm her. If Eden was taken back into its walls, there would be no escape.

This was her opportunity, her only chance. How many moonrises could she go without food? She was running out of time. Weakness filled up her bones, but she would have to find the strength.

She looked back at the sleeping spirits. Netty's eyes had opened and glowed against her indigo skin. Eden stared at the little girl, words unspoken. Netty didn't stir from the witch's embrace.

She had held Eden's warm, living hand. She was the lost spirit who the witch had saved. Netty had protected her. But Eden couldn't stay in Everdark. Not with the blowback of the witch's magic spreading on her skin. Eden only had two choices. She could stay in the world of the dead or escape back to the world of the living.

Eden stared into Netty's eyes one last moment before she took another step away from the little girl, away from the blanket.

Then she turned and ran.

Netty's screams filled the air, and Eden stumbled to the ground, gritty sand scraping her injured knee. She flew back upright and pounded down the beach.

"No!" Netty cried. "No, no, no! Come back!"

Eden pushed faster, tears leaking from her eyes, streaking down her face. The woods were so, so far away, but Eden continued to race down the beach. Goose bumps sprouted on her skin, bracing for the stabbing pain of the witch's long nails.

Netty's screams were fainter. The woods were close, closer still. Eden kept pounding, kept running. She could now see the tall trees and dense ferns. Eden never slowed, never stopped. Her breath came out in ragged gasps, and her feet burned in her boots.

The black beach sand gave way to brown soil and trees surrounded her. The smell of pine was sharp in her nose.

Eden didn't slow down when she entered the grove of trees. She kept her pace and the woods fully embraced her in their darkness.

CHAPTER TWENTY-ONE

Into the Woods

Netty's screams had stopped, and the woods were silent. Thick branches hid the moon. Eden leaned against the skinny trunk of a tall pine to catch her breath, lungs aching from the exertion of escape.

After resting a few moments, Eden ventured deeper into the woods. Resurrection ferns brushed against her long skirt, and Spanish bayonet leaves tugged at her sleeves. She longed for a flashlight, but her eyes eventually adjusted to the darkness.

The witch hadn't pursued her into the woods, and Eden wondered why. Netty's screams still echoed in her head, and she knew that the little girl's voice would haunt her.

She wove her way through the woods, the trees dense and close, like blades of grass. Darkness hid any clues of where she was going. She took off her gloves and inspected several trunks, hoping the fuzzy touch of moss could guide her north to Willow Hammock.

The surroundings came alive with sound as Eden explored under the heavy, wide branches of ancient live oaks. She placed her boots carefully on the ground, prodding for any roots that might trip her. Ferns trembled with hidden creatures, and when something scurried across her boot, Eden covered her mouth to stifle a scream.

The chittering of small animals grew louder high in the trees and low in the ferns. A quick dart of a fluffy tail caught Eden's attention, and she exhaled a sigh of relief. Small creatures with white-tipped fur darted up the trees in robotic spurts. Everdark squirrels.

Eden continued on her path while the noises intensified. Croaks of frogs and splashes in unseen water. Sharp caws from above on dark wings. A symphony of crickets. Familiar night sounds that had lulled her to sleep in her great-aunt's guest room. The squirrels followed her, traveling from branch to quivering branch. Eden felt the unease of other camouflaged creatures watching her.

She gathered the folds of her long skirt, so she could move faster in her boots. The woods had not harmed her, and a small inkling of hope spread on her skin like a warm salve. Maybe she would find her way back to Aunt Susanna's house after all.

The trees were now farther apart, a mix of red cedar, sweet gum, and magnolia. The sharp scent was fresh and soothing. Eden's boots treaded softly on thick layers of pine needles. Shoving branches out of her way, she continued forward, although she was unsure if she was going the right way. Behind her, a loud rustle made her pause. A different sound from the squirrels.

When she heard the noise again, it wasn't behind her but to her left. Too big to be a squirrel or a frog or an owl. A cold trickle of fear went down her spine.

The shuffling continued, and ferns trembled with movement until a small doe appeared, ears twitching. Its fur was dusky in the low light of the woods. The doe galloped away, tussling with leaves and branches in its exit.

The moon penetrated through the thick ceiling of trees and covered the ground in bright spots of light. As she pressed on, the furtive shuffling of leaves returned.

Eden breathed slowly, trying to tamp down her fright. She tried to convince herself it was only another deer. But the woods were now silent. No chittering conversations from the squirrels. They were quiet on the branches, which meant a predator was in their midst.

A low growl rumbled behind her.

The patter of footsteps and heavy panting forced Eden to turn and face a hulking dark shape with pointy ears and red, glowing eyes. As big as a bear, the creature had dagger teeth and curved claws. The plat-eye looked the same as it had in her dream.

Eden stood for a moment, frozen with terror. She glanced at a live oak with its low branches. She hadn't climbed a tree in a long time, but she wasn't sure if she would be fast enough to escape to its safety.

The plat-eye lurked closer, the space between them growing smaller. Eden put her trembling hands out in front of her in a weak defense. When the monster dog lunged at her, Eden turned and fled. Leaves whipped her face and branches tore at her curls.

Terrible grunts and growls echoed through the woods, and Eden's imagination took control. The plat-eye would drag her down among the resurrection ferns and feast on her bright skin.

This had been the warning in Netty's screams. The reason why the witch hadn't pursued her. The spirits knew what dwelled in these woods. Eden would never find her way out. Not alive.

But she stumbled out of the woods to an unfamiliar stretch of beach. The moon was high and bright in the sky, the ocean dark and expansive.

The Everdark creature scrambled onto the beach. In the full brightness of the moon, its red eyes shone with malice. Eden lurched into the surf, the waves soaking her long skirt.

The monster dog barked, and Eden covered her ears to block the horrible sound. She continued to wade into the ocean, her teeth chattering at its brutal coldness.

A splash of water keep them away, Aunt Susanna had said.

Eden had more than a splash of water at her disposal. The red-eyed dog continued to growl, spitting out loud, sharp barks, but it didn't move any closer to the waves. Eden waded farther into the ocean, until she was waist deep. The water was her only protection, but she knew that she couldn't stay in its cold grasp forever.

Eden couldn't return to the woods with the plat-eye blocking her path. Her only option was a smaller island in the distance. She hadn't swum in the Cathedral Day School's pool in almost a year and had only waded in the shallow depths of the ocean, her parents too afraid of riptides and rogue waves. She had no real technique nor any tested endurance, and the dark mass of land looked very far away, but Eden unlaced her boots.

Eden's long skirt was heavy with water and her bare feet no longer touched the sandy bottom. A roll of waves pushed her underneath into darkness, but she surged back up to the surface, coughing salty water. She watched her boots float away with the ocean current.

The plat-eye patrolled the beach, the surf keeping it at bay on the black sand. Eden knew if she came back on land, the red-eyed dog would devour her.

Floating on the ocean's surface, she let the waves carry her farther from shore. Soon the plat-eye was only a tiny spot on the beach. Underneath the full moon, it howled in fury.

Eden trembled in the water, but then she took a deep breath and started to swim.

CHAPTER TWENTY-TWO

Pirate Island

Hard coughs racked Eden's chest as she tumbled onto the smaller island's shore. Her arms were sore from the countless strokes of her swim, legs wobbly and heavy. Dropping to her knees in gratitude, she grabbed a fistful of sand and pushed out a relieved whimper.

Several dead trees dotted the beach. The branches were bare and bleached, a collection of wooden bones. The sand was lighter, gray with flecks of white that glinted in the moonlight.

Falling onto her back, Eden gazed at the sky, full of familiar constellations. The moon was a glowing globe above her but slowly making its descent to the west. The main island loomed in the distance, its shore a faint, dark line of trees, the howls of the plat-eye now swallowed by the loud crash of ocean waves.

Eden had escaped. She was no longer a prisoner in the witch's mansion. A weak laugh of triumph erupted from her chest. She was still in Everdark, but now she was more determined than ever to find her way back to Willow Hammock. She thought of her father and relatives. Soon she would be reunited with them.

Eden raised her arm and gasped at the indigo shimmer fading from her skin. Hope blossomed in her heart. The witch's blowback was receding. Sitting up, she surveyed her surroundings. Maybe she could find a sliver of sunlight on this smaller island, a jagged opening that would lead her back to the world of the living.

She stood up but swayed when her vision blurred. She held her stomach as it roiled and bent over to vomit, but nothing came out except a trickle of bitter bile.

Another wave of nausea moved over her. Eden's escape had taken its toll on her body. Her clothes were drenched from the ocean, and the island winds made her teeth chatter. She touched her forehead, which felt warmer than usual.

Eden slowly lay back down on the beach, curling into a tight ball. Maybe she needed to rest first before exploring the island. Her eyelids grew heavy with exhaustion, and she drifted into a deep sleep.

Something jabbed against Eden's ribs, and she woke from her slumber. Two shadows hovered over her. The ground was hard and damp, and her hands were covered in sand. Slowly, she remembered what had happened. The woods, the ocean, and the escape from the plat-eye.

Eden frantically crawled from the shadows, too weak to run. The phantoms followed her, carrying long wooden sticks, but then the moon revealed what they were.

Two boys with faded indigo skin stood over her, their eyes glowing in the darkness. Bare chested, they wore ragged pants but no shoes, their feet sugared with gray-white sand. One looked to be a little older than Netty, while the other seemed to be the same age as Grace.

Eden recognized them immediately. Her mother had drawn these boys in her sketchbook.

"She ain't dead," the younger boy said.

Eden gaped at them, not speaking. The older boy lowered his stick.

"Easy now," he said. "Not gon' hurt you. Tell me straight, how you get here?"

Eden swallowed, her throat scratchy and raw. "I swam. A . . . a plat-eye was chasing me. I thought they were only in graveyards."

The older boy exchanged a worried look with the younger one. "Not the one Mother Mary got. He guard the woods behind the Big House."

"You lucky he ain't eat you," the younger one added.

Eden shuddered thinking about the plat-eye's dagger teeth. She didn't doubt the little boy's words.

"My name's Eden," she offered. "I ran away—escaped from Mother Mary. I . . . I'm trying to find my way back to Willow Hammock."

The boys shared cautious looks. Eden didn't know if she was considered an enemy or an ally.

"My name Lorenzo," the older boy finally said. "This my brother, Isaac."

"Nice to meet you both," Eden said.

"How Mother Mary catch you if you ain't dead?" Isaac blurted out.

Lorenzo gave his little brother a warning glance, but Isaac only shrugged his shoulders. "You wanna know it too. She ain't one of us."

"Mother Mary found me on the beach," Eden answered. "I was in the woods in Willow Hammock at first, but then I found a way here . . . it was a mistake."

The boys plodded a few paces down the beach from Eden. They huddled together, heads touching. Eden's fate was in their hands. When they finished their conversation, the brothers trotted back to her.

"You wanna come with us?" Lorenzo asked.

Eden quickly nodded and the older boy helped her up. She no longer felt sick to her stomach, and although she stumbled at first, she found her footing on the beach.

"We gon' take you to the hospital," Lorenzo said. "Find you some dry clothes."

"A hospital?" Eden asked.

"Ain't no real hospital no more," the older boy answered.

"Are there . . . more spirits here?"

"Nobody here but us," Isaac said. "Welcome to Pirate Island."

She walked with the brothers into the island's interior landscape. Eden had so many questions, but she knew that she would have to wait for answers. Right now, she would have to trust these new spirits.

The hospital didn't resemble any that Eden had ever seen.

It reminded her of the houses in Willow Hammock. A large triangle roof was positioned over a porch. Bigger than First Church, the hospital was constructed with whitewashed wood. Other smaller buildings were scattered beyond it, hidden by the shadows of trees, but the hospital was the largest structure.

The boys climbed the stairs, and Eden followed them through the front door. An open area held toppled desks and chairs, with discarded papers on the floor. The boys padded over the thick layers and traveled down one of the long hallways. Eden passed doors, each of them displaying a number painted in faded blue.

Lorenzo opened one with a painted 18 on the front. "This our room. Stay here," the older boy said. "We gon' fetch you some clothes."

When the brothers left, Eden sat on one of the small twin beds. It was the opposite of the mansion's north-wing bedroom. No silk-covered chair or gilded vanity. Only bare walls and sand-blasted floors.

Eden went to the window, which faced a grove of live oaks. Several large seashells were on the window's ledge. She placed one close to her ear and listened to the ocean's echo.

A few books were gathered in a small tower on the table between the beds. Warped by water, the pages were full of stained, unreadable ink. Examining the stiff spines, Eden couldn't make out any of the titles. She wondered why the brothers had kept these books in their room.

The moon was lower in the sky, the tree line dampening its light. Eden hoped Netty wasn't too sad. By now, the little girl was back inside the witch's mansion. Bull would be preparing supper. Grace would be changing into a party dress. What would the older girl think of Eden's escape when she found out? Would Grace be impressed with her bravery?

No, Eden thought. *She's probably thinks I'm dead and is shaking her head at my stupidity.*

Maybe all the spirits in the mansion believed she had been devoured by the plat-eye. Later tonight, the witch would take her lantern and venture into the darkness to search for Eden's bloody bones.

Lorenzo and Isaac returned to the room with arms full of clothes. Long shirts and wide pants. Eden doubted any of these items would fit her. At least not like the fine dresses she had worn in the mansion. These clothes wouldn't have the marvel of the witch's magic.

The boys spread the clothes out on one of the beds, and Eden picked the smallest shirt and shortest pants. She would most likely have to roll and cuff the clothes for a better fit, but they were dry and smelled of salt.

"Thank you," Eden said.

"Come out when you ready," Lorenzo said.

Eden took off her wet clothes. The bruise had disappeared from her arm, and she smiled at her unmarked brown skin. Her escape from the witch's mansion had freed her from its doomed magic and now she had a chance to find her way back home.

Her new garments fit as poorly as she expected. She left the room and walked down the hallway to the front entrance of the hospital. Scanning the papers strewn across the floor like trash, she bent down and picked up one of the faded sheets, thin and crisp in her fingers.

Eden scanned the medical records of a US Navy soldier named Tormand Sullivan being treated for yellow fever. Eden searched the floor for more papers. All of them were records of sick soldiers ranging in time from 1881 to 1908. She remembered

Uncle Willie mentioning a quarantine hospital on one of the smaller sister islands.

Pushing the hospital door open, she found the boys in front of an outside fireplace. Isaac passed kindling to his older brother, and Lorenzo stoked the fire in a square hole surrounded by an iron grate. A red brick chimney released curls of gray smoke that wafted up into the air.

Eden sat facing the blaze, welcoming the glow and warmth. These spirits had taken her in, and she gladly accepted their hospitality. Lorenzo continued to stoke the fire, the embers burning bold in the growing darkness. The moon would be setting soon, and then Everdark night would be upon them.

"Does Mother Mary know about you two?" Eden asked.

"She do," Lorenzo answered. "But she let us be."

"Did you know her . . . from before?" Eden asked.

Lorenzo sat next to his brother, the fire illuminating his face in the darkness. "We was here long before she come to this side."

"Do either of you know a girl named Netty?" she asked them.

"We know she stay in the Big House," Isaac said.

"She came here after the 1809 hurricane," Eden volunteered.

"Way before our time," Lorenzo said. "Our boat capsize in 1906."

Eden had assumed that the boys had died of yellow fever, since they dwelled at the hospital. "Why are you . . . still here?"

Isaac lowered his head and Lorenzo gave her a steely stare. "Our daddy worked at the hospital."

Eden's face burned. The question had opened a wound. She

remembered the dates on some of the medical records. The latest date she had found was 1908, so Lorenzo and Isaac's father may have still been working at the hospital after they perished.

"When we come here, we all got a choice." The older boy leaned forward, his eyes locking with hers. "We stay or we move on. Folks who stay be waiting on they blood kin. But when Mother Mary come here, she brung her magic. She the one who control Everdark. Nobody can leave now."

The witch had sacrificed the sun and corrupted this spirit world. She had trapped the elder spirits and prevented other spirits from moving on. This was bigger than Eden had imagined.

"No one can stop her?"

"Every spirit that come through she catch," the older boy answered. "She even catch you."

"Is . . . is your dad here?"

"No," Lorenzo said. "We was waiting for him. But he ain't never come."

The fire had removed the chill from Eden's skin, but she still shivered at the reach of the witch's power. She had escaped the mansion and its rot. Her bruised arm had healed. But her hope of returning to the world of the living now had a shaky foundation.

"I'm trying to get back to Willow Hammock," she whispered. "But I don't know the way."

The wood sizzled and popped in the silence, and the boys didn't offer any help. The brothers were also trapped in this spirit world. Growing alarm crept up Eden's throat, a building scream of anger and despair.

"Time for us to go fish," Lorenzo finally said. "You best come with us."

"I can stay here," Eden said.

"Night bring out a lot of things," Isaac cautioned. "Hospital don't provide no protection for bright folks."

A shiver went up Eden's spine. If deer and squirrels were in Everdark, then so were alligators, snakes, and other predators. Too many things that would love to take a bite out of her.

The boys shuffled around in the fire's glow, their bare backs displaying cords of small muscles as they gathered pails, rope, and nets. Isaac lit a lantern, and she followed the younger boy, with his older brother traveling behind her.

CHAPTER TWENTY-THREE
Night Fishing

Eden walked on an established dirt path that was pillow soft. Branches hovered over them, and she parted Spanish moss like thick curtains. Lorenzo and Isaac stayed silent during the journey.

The path led to a desolate stone harbor full of crumbling rocks. Eden touched the side of a collapsed wall. Uncle Willie had mentioned that a smaller sister island had once been home to a navy fort. Maybe this had been its location, and the broken wall was all that remained of it. A wooden boat was anchored on the rocky shore. The ocean was dark in the starlight, and there were no other landmasses in the distance. Eden was at the edge of the spirit world.

"This the east side of Pirate Island," Isaac stated. "Mother Mary never come this way."

Eden carefully navigated the rocks to the water's edge, using Lorenzo's lantern as a guide. The water lapped against Eden's toes, and she retreated from the cold. Her swim was still fresh in her memory.

Lorenzo and Isaac put their supplies in the boat. Isaac turned to her with a proud grin that revealed a missing front tooth. "Made this with our own hands."

Eden returned the little boy's smile. "Looks sturdy."

"Learned straight from our daddy's knee," Lorenzo said. "Hall family known for crafting boats."

Eden swallowed. These were Uncle Willie's people. He had come from a long line of seafarers and boat-makers.

"I've met some of your family."

Lorenzo nodded. "Sound about right if you come from Willow Hammock. Although you don't sound saltwater to me."

"I wasn't born on Safina Island," Eden said. "I was visiting from the mainland. One of your relatives, William Hall, married my great-aunt, Susanna Gardener."

Isaac stopped loading the boat. "We knew them Gardeners. Loved the land like we loved the ocean."

After the boys prepped the boat, Eden settled onto one of the small benches and Isaac sat across from her. Lorenzo pushed the boat into the water, jumping in and rowing them away from the rocky shore.

The ocean's surface reflected the starry sky, and the boys threw their nets into the water with heavy plops. Isaac leaned over the edge and watched them disappear.

"Never used to fish at night before," Lorenzo said. "But the peace be the same."

Pirate Island was now farther away, but Eden felt calm. The ocean was still and quiet. In the middle of the dark expanse, she was safe. The older boy stared out at the horizon, his face serene and deep in thought.

A low hum and whoosh of air broke the surface. A large, dark tail hovered in the air, followed by a smaller one. A geyser of water spouted with a low trumpet sound.

"Whales," Eden whispered in awe.

They came closer, twisting on their backs and revealing their white bellies. Eden marveled at their size. The mother whale swam under the boat, and Eden leaned over to look in anticipation. The baby whale followed, its smaller body churning in the water. They broke the surface again farther away, and Eden's heart swelled with joy watching the creatures.

"They always come and greet us," Isaac said.

Uncle Willie had told her about these whales. They were called "right whales" because they were docile and easy to kill, and their valuable baleen had once been used for umbrellas and corsets. Now they were endangered and the rarest of creatures, protected under state law. She was happy to see that in this spirit world, they were safe and thriving.

The ocean settled and returned to its glass surface, but a strange glow caught Eden's attention. The little boy was learning out of the boat, his hands stirring the water.

"Isaac." Lorenzo's voice was laced with warning.

The light skimmed and skipped in the water, rippling in different bright colors. Iridescent pulses surrounded the boat and turned the ocean a deep blue.

"She need to see," Isaac said.

Silver flashes of fins and rainbow whooshes of scales darted around them. A pod of dolphins swam toward the boat, their happy croaks traveling through the air.

Isaac met the dolphins with glee, patting their long noses as they broke the surface. They flipped high into the air before splashing back down into the ocean. The little boy laughed, deep and bright, like the light surrounding the boat. Eden joined him as she touched the rubbery skin of a dolphin, who whistled and clacked.

Lorenzo retrieved the nets, their catch swishing on the floor of the boat. Other fish leaped on deck, and the older brother quickly put them in pails of water. Isaac pulled his hands out of the ocean and the light dimmed, returning to dark glass. The dolphins chittered their goodbyes and dove back into the depths.

"My brother got a gift," Lorenzo said softly. "Mother Mary don't know. She can't never know."

The fire was still glowing when they returned to the hospital. Lorenzo stoked the flames while Isaac cleaned the fish. The boys put them on spiked sticks, cooking them in the fire. Eden's stomach growled and she quickly covered it to block the sound. But the little boy had heard. Isaac turned to her with a worried look on his face. Eden tried to give him a reassuring smile.

"It's okay," she said.

Lorenzo offered a cup of water, and Eden took a small sip. It wasn't as horrible as what she had drunk in the mansion, and Eden didn't know if it was because she was now used to the sour taste or if the witch's magic held less power on this island. She forced a few more swallows before coughing and then let her roiling stomach settle.

"Why is this place called Pirate Island?" Eden asked.

"Named after Teach the Terrible," Lorenzo said. "He come here to bury treasure."

"We been trying to find it," Isaac said. "But reckon them gold coins ain't gon' do much for us now."

The boys ate their fish in silence. Eden had declined their offer for food. She was afraid that she would only taste bitter ash. She averted her gaze from their dinner and stared at the hospital's porch, which glowed red from the firelight.

Eden thought of her father and relatives again. Had they stopped searching for her? Eden imagined them inside Aunt Susanna's mint-green house sitting at her kitchen table and grieving the girl who had come to her mother's birthplace only to be lost forever.

They watched the fire until it burned to its embers, the darkness closing in on them. When the fire died into gray ashes, Lorenzo sat next to Eden, his face blended with the darkness, eyes glowing with grave concern.

"Time ain't long for you in this world," he said.

Eden nodded, the truth too unbearable to speak.

"Reckon we can help you," he said.

Hope bloomed again in Eden's heart, a tiny, strong sprout. "You . . . you know the way to Willow Hammock?"

Lorenzo shook his head, confusing Eden. But then Isaac moved beside her, his small hands touching her arm, solid and cold. The same hands that had conjured light in the ocean.

"We ain't know the way," he said. "But we can take you to the one who do."

CHAPTER TWENTY-FOUR

The Frost House

They returned to the beach where Eden had first drifted ashore, the bone trees now barely visible in the starlight. Lorenzo pulled a wooden boat from underneath a pile of dried ferns. The boys placed it on their shoulders and ushered it down to the waves. Eden held the lantern and stepped on board. Isaac helped his brother push the boat into the surf.

The older boy worked the oars, his shoulders and arms flexing with the exertion. Isaac skimmed the surface with his fingers and hummed, but no light appeared beneath his touch.

Lorenzo steered them away from the main island's shoreline and rowed farther north. The sky was radiant with stars and a meteor streaked across the sky, disappearing below the tree line. Eden closed her eyes and made a wish. More than ever she wanted to be reunited with her father. She wanted to hug Natalie again. She wanted to go home.

The main island's beach disappeared, replaced by cypress and willow trees meeting the water. Lorenzo guided the boat through marshland onto a wide river.

"Dim the lantern," he instructed his younger brother.

Eden shivered as the river grew narrow and trees crept over them, blocking out the starlight. Lorenzo guided the boat to a small wooden wharf, where it knocked against the platform and bobbed in the water. Isaac helped Eden onto the landing while Lorenzo tied up the boat.

"Stay close," Lorenzo said. "Lot of things lurking after dark."

The woods made Eden's pulse race as she remembered the plat-eye and its terrifying howls. Lorenzo's lantern guided them to a well-worn path, and they came upon an open field where a tiny house was covered in frost. In its island surroundings, the ice looked out of place, and Eden stared in wonder.

"Stay here with Isaac. Let me tell the story." The older boy walked toward the house.

"My brother will make it right," Isaac whispered.

When the older boy approached the porch, the door opened and a fire's glow spilled out into the darkness. Eden held her breath as she waited. She hoped that whatever story Lorenzo was telling would bring her the help she needed.

Lorenzo finally motioned them to come forward. Eden and Isaac crossed the field to the porch steps, which were slick with ice. Eden carefully walked inside the house.

A young girl was stoking a small fire in a wood-burning stove that stood in the middle of the room. She had the shimmering indigo skin of an Everdark spirit but seemed to be about Eden's age. Her gingham dress was plain and her hair was hidden beneath a white head wrap. She met Eden's eyes and gave her a warm smile.

"Don't see bright girls around here much," she said.

She returned the young girl's smile. "I'm Eden."

"My name Ruby." The young girl offered her hand, and Eden took it, now familiar with the coldness.

"You can take me back to Willow Hammock?"

The girl gave a quick nod. "I know the way."

Lorenzo leaned on the wall next to the door. "Ruby, you sure about this?"

"I can take her when the moon come up," Ruby confirmed. "No need to run into Mother Mary tonight."

The older boy stood tense by the door, as if not totally convinced. Eden walked toward him.

"I'll be fine," she reassured him.

"Be careful," he said.

Isaac moved beside his older brother, his wide eyes glowing against his skin. He was the little boy who could conjure light in a world of darkness. It didn't seem fair he would remain trapped here after she returned to the world of the living, but Eden couldn't help him. She couldn't help any of these spirits.

"Thanks for everything," Eden told the brothers. "I couldn't have made it here without your help. I don't know what I would have done if you two hadn't come for me."

"You be back with your people soon." Lorenzo took Isaac's hand and lifted his gaze to Ruby. "Best take care of her."

"On my sister's name, it be done," the young girl said.

Satisfied with Ruby's answer, Lorenzo nodded and the boys left.

The wood-burning stove clicked with heat as Eden sat in front of it, watching the flames. She had traveled farther north. Perhaps she was already in Everdark's version of Willow Hammock. Maybe in this place of eternal night, Ruby would take her to a replica of Aunt Susanna's mint-green house. Could it be as simple as opening a door back to the living world?

A faint howl interrupted Eden's thoughts.

"Don't worry none about that plat-eye. He soon find something to keep him occupied," Ruby said.

"He's probably still looking for me." Eden shuddered.

The young girl worked around the room, straightening jars on a far shelf and sweeping the floor. When she was done, she put a dinged kettle of water on the stove. Ruby settled beside Eden, the glow of the fire illuminating her indigo skin.

"Lorenzo told me you was a Gardener," Ruby stated as she appraised her.

Eden nodded. "My mom was a Gardener."

"Thought every Gardener girl was full of magic." Ruby frowned.

Eden thought of Miss Nadine. On Loretta Beach, the elder claimed she had seen the shine on Eden's skin, but here in Everdark, no one saw any magic.

"So where Mother Mary catch you?" the young girl finally asked.

"She found me on the beach."

Ruby huffed in disgust. "Don't surprise me none. She hunt at night. Even though you ain't got no shine, you still a bright girl."

"Why aren't you in the mansion?" Eden asked.

Ruby shrugged her shoulders. "Mother Mary ain't got no need for me."

"Do you know Netty and Grace?"

The young girl stared at the fire flickering behind the iron grate. Eden wondered if she had made another blunder. If she had asked this spirit the wrong question.

"Ain't know them in life," Ruby finally answered. "But know them well enough dead."

The kettle's loud whistle made Eden jump. Ruby let out a chuckle and removed it from the stove's heat.

"Bet you done seen a lot in that Big House." She sprinkled a small pinch of leaves and spices into a tin cup and then poured in hot water. Steam rose in tiny white curls. "Drink this."

Eden's stomach clenched. "I can't."

"You can," Ruby corrected her. "This water different. Come from my sister's well."

Eden took the tin cup from Ruby's hand. She didn't want to drink the tea that this spirit had made. She didn't want to taste the rancid water.

"Ain't tainted," Ruby reassured her.

Eden tentatively put the tin cup to her lips, taking a small sip. When she finally swallowed, she widened her eyes in surprise. Sweetness covered her tongue with traces of nettle and cinnamon.

"Told you." Ruby smiled. "Drink some more."

Eden drank all Ruby's tea, the warmth flowing through her veins and soothing her aching body.

"Moon sleeping now. You should get some rest too."

Eden stretched out on a thick pallet on the floor. Ruby gave her a feathered pillow and a thick quilt that smelled of sage.

"Ease your burden for a spell," the young girl said. "We be on our way when the moon wake up."

CHAPTER TWENTY-FIVE

Last Moonrise

After a few hours of dreamless sleep, Eden blinked awake, first unaware of her surroundings. Then she remembered meeting the brothers on Pirate Island. The beautiful whales and joyful dolphins. Isaac's deep-blue magic. Her memory told her that she was now in the house covered in frost.

Ruby was sitting in front of the wood-burning stove. She now wore a gray day dress with long sleeves. The young girl's head was uncovered, her hair neatly braided in two long plaits. Eden examined her arm again, and the shimmering bruise hadn't returned. Her skin was still brown and unmarked, and she released a sigh of deep relief.

Hearing Eden stir on the pallet, Ruby turned to her. "We gon' be on our way soon."

She put the dented kettle on the stove, and the rumbling boil of water was the only noise in the house. At the kettle's loud whistle, Ruby made another batch of tea. Slowly enjoying the clean and crisp taste, Eden closed her eyes as she sipped.

Ruby presented her with a soft cotton day dress that was slightly too big for her, but it was better than the ill-fitting shirt and pants she currently wore. She also gave Eden a pair of old, worn boots. Eden tied a knot at the dress hem so she wouldn't trip. She couldn't wait to return to the world of the living, to her jeans and T-shirts, the kind of clothes that the witch thought were a disgrace and had burned in the mansion's fireplace.

Eden sat next to Ruby on the floor, facing the stove. "I hope this won't get you in trouble."

"Won't be no trouble." Ruby gave a weak smile that didn't reach her eyes.

Eden wondered if Ruby's sister was one of the spirits that the witch had captured. If she was one of the whispers she'd heard in the lower levels of the mansion. Maybe this was why Lorenzo had believed Ruby when she said she would escort Eden back to Willow Hammock.

"What's your sister's name?" Eden asked.

"Ade. But she more like my mama than my sister. She the one who raised me," the young girl said quietly. "This her house."

"Why is it covered in frost?" Eden asked.

"Winter don't come much, but one time ice come strong on Safina. Ade got sick, but she didn't have no money to get to the mainland and see a doctor."

Eden stared at the spirit lost in memory. The young girl's eyes filled with tears, but none fell down her cheeks. Ruby's grief was understated and managed. On the brink of crying, but never surrendering to the tears. Eden knew this control of sadness.

"Did you . . . get sick too?" Eden asked gently.

Ruby swallowed her grief. "No, my sister die in 1931. I come here in 1936. But she waited for me."

Eden quickly calculated all the death time frames she had collected in Everdark. Besides the witch, Ruby was the youngest spirit she had met.

"Was Mother Mary here?" she asked.

"Yes," Ruby hissed. "She was laying tricks for the Big House when I come here. Then stole my sister from me."

A familiar surge of anger heated Eden's face. The witch was keeping the young girl's sister as a prisoner in the mansion. She had tried to steal Eden's life by keeping her in Everdark. They had the same enemy.

The first rays of moonlight filtered through the window, and the house filled up with pale silver light. Eden thought of the wish she had made earlier on the shooting star. If fulfilled, this would be her last moonrise in Everdark.

Ruby stood up and smoothed out her dress. "We best be leaving now."

Eden followed Ruby out to the icy porch as the young girl adjusted a wool shawl around her. The moon had risen over the top of the pine trees, and Eden carefully inched down the slick steps, holding tight to the porch's rail.

"Mighty sure Mother Mary been looking for you," Ruby said.

The young girl ventured toward the field. Now in the bright light of the moon, Eden could see the house's paint under the ice, a faded peeling pink.

Eden followed the spirit across the field to a dirt road, similar to the one that she had traveled in Uncle Willie's truck. Thinking of her great-uncle, with his warm, musical voice, released a twinge of ache in Eden's chest, but soon she would hear his voice again.

The sour smell of the marsh hinted that they were forging farther north. Eden crossed her arms for warmth. Ruby walked purposefully down the road, confident of the destination. But abruptly, she stopped. Eden had to swerve to the young girl's side to keep from bumping into her.

"Why did we—"

"Go! Hide!"

Ruby's frightened voice silenced her quickly. Eden ran into the tall grass and pressed her chest to the ground. She peeked from her hiding place. A large bird had blocked Ruby's path. But it wasn't a normal bird. Eden guessed it was at least ten feet tall. A mountain of danger. Although the creature's head was bare and blood red, dark feathers covered the rest of its body, and its jointed legs ended in sharp claws. She remembered her mother's drawings in the sketchbook. Aunt Susanna's island story of Old Buzzard. Netty's warnings that the god-spirit was here in Everdark. Eden trembled in the tall grass.

"Old Buzzard, I got the right of way," Ruby said. "Ain't interested in what you offering."

The god-spirit cocked his head, as if understanding the young girl's words. Slowly, he spread his wings, which spanned the width of the road, and scratched the ground with his claws. Whorls of dust rose around the creature.

Ruby backed away as he stalked toward her. Swaying back and forth on his legs, the creature let out a loud caw, bold and wicked. Ruby slammed to the ground, her head bowed in reverence. Old Buzzard loomed over her, pecking at the young girl's hair. Ruby cried out in fear.

Eden pressed her body lower to the ground, holding her breath as the god-spirit took to the sky, circling low. She shivered like prey in the tall grass, but Old Buzzard flew away and disappeared into the trees.

Ruby called to Eden. "You can come out now."

Eden stood up, shaking, and returned to the road. "Is this the crossroads?"

"Ain't no crossroads here," Ruby said flatly. "Old Buzzard think I'm getting weak is all. I ain't accepting his offer."

Eden searched the star-filled sky again, but the god-spirit didn't return. They continued down the dirt road and then veered into another field toward the woods. Through the treetops, Eden saw a flash of white. She quickly retraced her steps, and a church steeple revealed itself among the foliage.

"Is First Church here?" Eden asked.

Irritation appeared on Ruby's face. "That ain't the way."

Doubt stirred in Eden's chest. "My aunt's house isn't far from the church."

"Maybe in your bright world, but not here. Didn't I say I know the way? You want my help or not?"

The nagging feeling in Eden's chest grew, but she swallowed the doubt and let it bubble in the pit of her stomach. "I do want your help," she finally said.

Ruby moved through the field and into the woods, and Eden quickly followed her.

Eden's experience in the woods had been full of terror and danger. Her pulse quickened as branches hovered over them. Ruby moved between the trees, resurrection ferns brushing the hem of her dress.

"Why couldn't we stay on the road?" Eden asked.

"Quicker this way," Ruby answered. "You seen what be on the road. Best not meet Old Buzzard again."

Eden shivered at the memory of the god-spirit, with his sharp claws. The danger was real, but she wanted to get back to the world of the living, so she took a deep breath and gathered her courage.

Ruby walked in careful steps, and Eden followed her lead. The woods were quiet. No squirrels chittered in the branches. An eerie feeling of wrongness filled Eden's senses.

Silence laced through the trees, and her doubt eased back into her throat, settling on her tongue. Did Ruby know where she was going? Maybe the young girl didn't know the way. Maybe she had forgotten.

Leaves rustled ahead of them, and both girls stopped at the sound. A small, dark figure emerged from a cluster of Spanish bayonets, and two goldenrod eyes stared at them. The black cat hissed at Ruby.

The young girl picked up a small branch and wielded it like a wooden sword. "You, get! Get out of my way!" she yelled.

The black cat hissed again, dodging the young girl's swings before darting away. Eden grabbed Ruby's arm.

"Stop! I know that cat!"

Ruby dropped the branch, and Eden searched the woods for a glimpse of shiny fur or swishing tail. The black cat had been looking for her, and now Ruby had chased it away.

Eden's doubt tumbled out of her mouth. "I have to go find that cat."

The young girl stopped walking but didn't turn around. "We almost there."

Furtive movements shook the nearby bushes, and dark shadows flitted among the branches. Then Eden heard the low rumble of a growl. An eerie coldness slid down her neck, a feeling of being watched by the plat-eye, biding its time. She could go search for the black cat, but it would be at her own peril.

The mortal danger of the plat-eye was real, and Eden wasn't sure if she would be able to escape again. Ruby told her that they were close, so Eden swallowed her doubts once more.

The young girl ventured deeper into the woods until they grew sparse and led to a thick grove of orange trees. A pulse of vague memory flowed through Eden. She plodded on an old seashell path overgrown with wiry stalks of weeds and wildflowers. The faint smell of salt filled the air. In the distance, she saw a gurgling fountain with a marble angel in its center. Bright white columns flickered bright against the darkness of the trees.

She had returned to the witch's mansion.

Eden jerked to run back into the woods, but Ruby grasped her arms, holding them tight and strong. "Hold still now."

"You lied to me," Eden spat.

Ruby dragged her onto the grand lawn past the majestic fountain. The front doors of the mansion opened, and the witch walked onto the portico. Still as beautiful as ever, her eyes glowed against her indigo skin.

The Witch of Everdark gave Eden a cruel smile. "Welcome back home, daughter."

CHAPTER TWENTY-SIX

Broken Promise

The witch glided down the mansion's stairs. Her hair was still in the thick braid, although long wisps had escaped and framed her face. She was dressed in the same blouse and brown skirt from the beach picnic. Eden stared warily at the witch's long, sharp nails.

"Been looking all over for you." The witch's voice was full of concern. "Mighty afraid you was took from us."

Eden squirmed in Ruby's cold grip. She didn't care that the witch had been worried about her welfare. The young girl had tricked her. In the woods, the black cat had tried to warn her, Eden was certain of that now. She remained silent, with an angry glare.

The witch tilted her head in amusement. "Why you so cross, bright girl? You better be glad Ruby was the one who found you instead of my plat-eye. He always hungry. Just knew I was gon' find you in them woods torn to pieces."

When Ruby let go of her arm, Eden stumbled forward, hating the spirit who had betrayed her.

The witch turned back to the mansion's front doors. "Grace, I know you spying. Make yourself known."

The older girl slowly walked out onto the portico. Grace's

hair was braided in tight cornrows, and she wore a simple day dress of green-striped cotton. She stood next to the witch on the portico, staring at Eden in surprise.

Eden looked past the older girl to the gilded glass doors, but Netty never appeared. Regret twisted in her chest.

"We thought you was dead," Grace said.

"Had us all filled up with worry," the witch agreed. "Ruby, you should have brung her straight to me."

The young girl shuffled, wrapping her shawl tighter around her shoulders. "Found her late last moon in the woods, all muddy and such. Cleaned her up best I could. But you right, Mother Mary. Your plat-eye woulda caught her if it weren't for me."

Ruby was lying to the witch. She hadn't mentioned Lorenzo and Isaac. The brothers were the ones who had found her. They had told her that Eden had escaped the plat-eye and swum to Pirate Island. But it didn't matter why Ruby lied. She had proven herself untrustworthy. The young girl had betrayed Eden and brought her back to this awful place. A sudden wave of nausea hit Eden.

The witch surveyed the clothes Eden wore with disdain. "So you took her in for the night. Guess I should be thanking you for taking care of my daughter."

"Need more than a thank-you," Ruby said. "I remember what we done agreed on. You promised me a trade if I brung you a bright girl. Now here one is right in front of you."

Grace let out a sigh and folded her arms, and Ruby sneered at her. There was an unspoken history between these two spirits, but Eden didn't care why they didn't like each other. She didn't care if they were enemies. Neither one had helped her. She was still here in this spirit world.

A low fever rose in Eden's body, a shroud of heat that made her weak. Eden looked down at her hand and shuddered. Shimmering in the moonlight, her fingers were a dark shade of indigo, her nails pitch-black.

The witch turned her full attention to Ruby. "I don't remember no trade. My daughter ain't barter."

Ruby's jaw tightened, and she lifted her chin in defiance. "Don't act like you don't remember nothing. I done delivered on my end. You best give me my sister."

The witch gave Ruby a cold smile, showing all her teeth. "Your sister where she belong."

When Ruby lunged at the witch, Grace blocked her path. The two spirits struggled, all flailing arms and grunts as they tumbled down the stairs onto the grand lawn. Grace finally overpowered the younger girl, pinning her down in front of Eden.

"You forget your place," the witch said in a dark tone.

Ruby struggled again until she rolled on top of Grace, and then scrambled toward the fountain, grasping her torn shawl. "Your word ain't nothing, you leech!"

Grace rose and bolted to gather the younger spirit in her arms. Ruby struggled against her, and the girls thrashed again. Ruby yelled and punched, a reaction to the witch's betrayal. Now maybe the young girl knew how it felt having something promised snatched away.

"Grace, stop fighting like an alley cat," the witch finally said. "Leave her be."

Ruby scurried away on her hands and knees, but then she froze as if under a spell. Wisps of black smoke surrounded her. The witch sauntered down the stairs and crossed the grand lawn. Ruby whimpered in fright as the witch loomed over her.

"You have no respect." The witch's voice was laced with venom, a dangerous warning. "The only promise I done made was to your sister. I promised Ade to let you go free. Now you come to my house and insult me?"

"Ain't your house," Ruby panted.

The witch's eyes turned solid black as she raised her hands in the air. Winds slashed through the trees and clouds hid the moon, shrouding them in darkness. Ruby clawed at her neck, gasping and laboring to breathe.

Grace moved beside Eden and took her bruised hand, the coldness stark against her rising fever. "You gon' see what happens when you make Mother Mary cross," the older girl said.

The witch's voice was now a thunderous echo. "You deserve to stay like this until you respect me, but since your brung my daughter home, I'm full of forgiveness."

The witch lowered her hands, and the brightness returned to her eyes. Parting clouds revealed the moon, and its silver light spilled onto the mansion's grand lawn.

"Get off my land, girl," the witch hissed. "Pray I forget your insolence."

On shaky limbs, Ruby collected her torn shawl. Her eyes brimmed with tears that trailed down her cheeks. She gave Eden one last pleading look before she cowered and lumbered down the seashell path, disappearing into the orange grove.

"Mother Mary, why you letting her leave?" Grace shrieked.

"You know that girl an empty husk," the witch replied. "Ruby can't do nothing for me. She need to take Old Buzzard's offer so we can be rid of her."

Ruby had been Eden's last chance. Her skin was already changing, the brightness of life draining away. There wouldn't be another escape.

A scorching heat raged inside her body. Blood red crept into her vision. Grace's frantic voice sounded far away, but Eden could no longer speak. She lost her balance, surrendered to the fever, and fell into darkness.

CHAPTER TWENTY-SEVEN
Bound Spirits

Eden stirred beneath a quilt in the north-wing bedroom. She was wearing a nightgown with a delicate lace neckline. The same one she had worn the first time she woke up in Everdark.

Grace was sitting on the bed next to her, but the older girl wasn't frowning. Her face was filled with worry and concern. On the other side of the bed, Netty stood, looking stricken and afraid. Tears sparkled in the little girl's eyes, but she remained silent.

"Fever raged you good," the older girl said. "Seem you done made it out now."

"How long was I asleep?" Eden asked, her voice raspy.

"Two moons," Grace answered.

The room was bright with silver light. Two more moonrises. Now Eden couldn't remember how long she had been in this world. Time had lost all meaning.

"Where's Mother Mary?" Eden asked.

"She downstairs with Bull," Grace said.

"Good," Eden said quickly. "I don't want her to know I'm awake. I have to leave now."

"You ain't going nowhere," Grace said.

"I have to leave," Eden repeated. "When I was with Ruby, I saw First Church, which means I can find my great-aunt's house. Maybe in the woods I can find—"

Suddenly Netty burst into tears. The little girl's cries bounced around the room in sad waves.

Eden tried to comfort the little girl shaking with grief. "Netty, I can't stay here. I'll miss you, but I have to leave."

The older girl's face was now full of sympathy, a bearer of bad news. "You can't leave. Too late for you."

Eden let out a shaky breath and slowly pulled down the quilt to reveal her hands. Both of them were deep indigo and shimmered in the moonlight. She let out an alarmed cry and frantically pushed her legs out of the quilt. The deep-brown shade of her skin was gone. She fumbled with the nightgown, the seams stretching and ripping as she searched her body.

Eden's skin revealed what had happened. She had been marked by the blowback of the witch's stolen magic. She was no longer a bright girl. Eden was now a spirit of Everdark.

"When?" she whispered.

"I brung you here right after you fell," Grace replied. "Netty tried to take care of you. Nothing she could do."

Eden glanced at the little girl crying next to the bed. Netty had tried to protect her, but she had been powerless.

She would never see her father again. Or Natalie. She would never see Aunt Susanna or Uncle Willie. None of her Safina Island relatives. All that had been taken from her. She was bound to Everdark now. Forever. *Always.*

Eden's scream was loud and shattering, a feral roar. She

drew the sound from the pit of her stomach and it riled up in angry torrents, scorching her lungs and ripping out of her throat.

Unfazed by her emotional distress, Grace stood up from the bed. "You one of us now." The older girl walked to the door and gave Netty a lingering look before leaving the room.

Eden scooted to the side of the bed where Netty stood crying. She touched the little girl's hand, which was solid but no longer cold. As an Everdark spirit, Eden didn't have the warmth of life in her veins.

"I'm sorry for leaving you on the beach," Eden whispered. "I know you don't like that word, but it's the only one I can say to you."

Netty sniffed and squeezed Eden's hand. "Sorry too."

She embraced Netty in a fierce hug. Eden smoothed the little girl's coiled hair, feeling the dampness of tears on her nightgown. When Netty stopped crying, they lay together on the bed, unmoving. Two dead girls finding comfort in each other.

"Ain't mad at you for leaving," Netty whispered against Eden's chest. "Thought you was worse than dead."

"Ruby tricked me." A boil of anger flared up in Eden's face. The young girl had made a promise to Lorenzo and Isaac. The brothers would have never gone to Ruby for help if they knew she would betray Eden.

Netty let out a sad sigh. "Ruby only done that to save her sister."

"I died because of her," Eden snapped, her anger still raw.

"Only Ade can help you," Netty said. "Ruby was trying to get her back."

Eden didn't care anymore. None of it mattered now. She could never return to the world of the living. She stared at the unblemished ceiling. But as she steadied her gaze, the mirage shimmered and the rot appeared, fully covering the ceiling. Eden studied the north-wing bedroom, and the decay had also overtaken the walls, quivering like a living thing. The witch's magic was failing.

"When you first come here, I remember you," Netty whispered, a bare wisp of air. "Seen you in my dream. Told you to stay away."

Eden closed her eyes. She remembered the dark dream on the moonless beach. Netty had tried to warn her, but the lure of Everdark had been too strong, the revelation of its magic too much to ignore. Eden's deep curiosity had brought her to this spirit world, and now she had paid the ultimate price.

She hugged the little girl tighter in her arms. "This isn't your fault."

"Ade helped a bright girl leave Everdark," Netty whispered, the light air of her words brushing Eden's skin. "Only strong magic can push back into the living world. When Mother Mary found out, she brung Ade here. Took her shine."

Eden leaned closer to Netty's ear. "Did you meet the bright girl?"

Netty shook her head. "Bull told me you the first Gardener to come here in many moons. Ain't never been one in the mansion."

"How did Mother Mary find out about Ade's magic?" Eden asked.

"Grace told her." Netty's whispers turned sharp. "She spy on us and tell Mother Mary. I thought she was my sister."

Eden remembered the little girl's warning about Grace. Was the older girl listening to them now? Spying on them for the witch? She leaned closer to Netty's ear, her faint words barely audible.

"Did Bull tell you the bright girl's name?" she asked. "The one who escaped?"

"Nora," Netty answered.

The revelation sounded true in Eden's bones. Her mother had been the last Gardener girl who had traveled between worlds.

"I'm Nora's daughter," Eden whispered in Netty's ear.

CHAPTER TWENTY-EIGHT
Child of Everdark

Netty left Eden alone in the north-wing bedroom with her thoughts. She spent most of the day staring at the ruined ceiling. Tendrils of rot crept like hungry vines over the door, twisting around the crystal doorknob. The mansion's beauty was disappearing. The blowback was growing stronger.

Eden finally changed into the day dress with the mother-of-pearl buttons and sat in front of the vanity mirror. She still had the same eyes that tilted up at the corners. Full lips and sharp cheekbones inherited from her mother. Loose curls and thick eyebrows like her father. But Eden's skin was like an Everdark sky scattered with stardust.

She put her hand over her heart. There was no beating rhythm underneath her fingers, only stillness. She inhaled deeply, filling up her lungs with air before releasing it in a soft whistle. Everdark spirits could sleep, they could eat, and they could cry, but their hearts didn't stir.

She walked to the window, and the courtyard stood before her. The seashell path leading to the ocean reflected brilliant white underneath the moon. Now that she was a spirit, this would be one of her eternal views.

A deep rumble of rage rattled her bones.

Eden returned to sit in front of the vanity mirror, forever dead. She blinked at the painful prick of tears.

The door cracked open, and Eden straightened up in the silk-covered chair. But instead of Netty appearing, the witch entered the north-wing bedroom.

Eden stiffened when the witch stood behind her, their eyes meeting in the vanity mirror. The witch's hair was pressed into long ringlets, and she wore an ivory dress with an intricate seed-pearl design. Draped in diamonds and emeralds, she perfectly embodied a movie star going to a party. Eden realized it was the first time she had seen the witch since she'd fainted on the grand lawn. She was still the most beautiful woman Eden had ever seen.

"You want me to help you get ready for supper?" The witch's voice was pleasant and soothing. The question was harmless enough, but Eden didn't think she would be allowed to refuse, so she said nothing.

The witch went to the wardrobe and pulled out a pale yellow dress. She laid it carefully on the bed along with a ruffled crinoline slip.

"Renata Spelling doted on her nieces," she said. "Dresses from New York City and Paris. Anything to lure them to the island, but them girls would never stay for long."

The witch sat on the bed, admiring the radiant-colored dress. Her eyes were downcast, as if remembering a past disappointment.

"Did you know I died twice?" the witch asked. "They made me a casket. Baby-sized. Didn't get no funeral because I had other plans. Weren't ready to be dead yet, you see. Maybe been better if I stayed that way the first time."

Eden twisted one of the mother-of-pearl buttons on her day dress and listened.

"I was born with a caul. Elders called it a veil," the witch continued. "Midwife shook it off me, and my mama put it in one of her jars. When it turn silver, she told me as a seventh daughter, I came into the world with a strong gift. Probably the reason why I came back. Too much shine to waste."

"You were full of magic." The words slipped out of Eden's mouth before she could stop herself.

The witch huffed at her response. "Most Turner women known to lay a powerful trick. But nobody could lay a trick like me. My sisters was mighty jealous because Mama thought my gift would save us all. When I found out harming paid more than healing, well, they didn't take too kindly to that. Didn't want no part of it. But all that money got me away from Safina. After that I didn't lay another trick. Didn't wanna hurt nobody else. But when I come back, folks expected me to go back to my old ways."

The witch stood up with the dress and slip in her hands. Eden took the garments from her without a word and ventured behind the dressing screen. When she returned wearing the perfectly tailored dress with the crinoline slip fluttering underneath, the witch was glaring at the ceiling. Eden remembered what Netty had told her on the beach. *Sometime I find Mother Mary in a room with a bad look on her face.*

Eden knew the witch could see the blowback's decay in the

north-wing bedroom. It was in every crack and crevice, proof that her stolen magic was fading.

When she stood in front of her, the witch averted her gaze from the ruined ceiling and appraised Eden in approval.

"You the prettiest daughter," she said. "You my favorite."

Eden wondered if the witch could still push her down into darkness. Could the witch's sharp nails prick her dead skin and unleash her magic?

She remembered the power that the witch had wielded over Ruby on the mansion's grand lawn. The frantic whispers behind the locked doors in the lower levels.

Slowly Eden sat in front of the silk-covered chair as the witch selected a double-strand pearl necklace and garnet earrings. She didn't seem to mind Eden's silence. The witch sang the melody of "Cheek to Cheek" as she styled Eden's hair in a high bun, adorning it with golden flower pins. Eden couldn't feel any coldness in the witch's fingers, only a loving touch.

When the witch finished, she escorted Eden down the spiral staircase through the library to the great room, with its familiar trappings. In the grand dining room, Grace and Netty were already seated in their party dresses and jewels.

"So happy tonight," the witch announced at the head of the table. She brushed her long hair from her shoulders and rang a dainty silver bell.

Bull shuffled into the room. Wearing his white servant jacket, he rolled his cart to the dining table. His penny eyes flashed in the moonlight. When he saw Eden, he paused for a moment but recovered his stiff stature.

"My daughter done come back to me." The witch beamed. "We all together again at supper."

Bull wouldn't meet Eden's eyes and silently placed the appetizer dishes of cucumber sandwiches and shrimp cocktail on the dining table before shuffling back to the kitchen.

The girls nibbled on the appetizers, but Eden didn't feel the ache of hunger as she had as a bright girl. Her stomach didn't rumble. When Bull returned with the main course and placed the silver-domed plate in front of her, Eden finally picked up her fork for a taste.

An explosion of flavor filled her mouth. The beef tips were tender and the gravy seasoned with garlic and peppercorn. Eden used her fork to swivel the new potatoes in their basting of butter and herbs. The asparagus gave a satisfying crunch between her teeth. For dessert, Bull served her a caramel roll with an extra scoop of ice cream, and it melted cold and sweet on her tongue.

She hated herself for enjoying the meal.

After Bull cleared the dishes, the witch stood up from her position at the head of the table.

"Tonight been a celebration of my beloved daughter Eden." The witch's beauty was illuminated under the dining room skylights. "But we got another thing to celebrate. The power of true love."

Eden exchanged confused looks with Netty and Grace.

The witch rang the bell again and Bull reappeared. But this time, he wasn't alone. A tall figure stood beside him, hidden in the shadows of the doorway.

At first, Eden thought it was Renata Spelling, but that

couldn't be right. The witch would never invite the mansion's former owner to supper.

When Bull escorted the stranger into the grand dining room, the moonlight revealed a teenage boy, draped in an elegant velvet suit, his skin the color of indigo. It was another Everdark spirit.

Grace sprang from her chair, knocking it to the floor. A cry escaped her lips as she rushed to the teen boy, wrapping her arms around him, though he didn't respond to Grace's shouts of joy.

Eden now realized who the stranger was standing stiff in the older girl's arms. It was Almond. The boy Grace loved.

In the icy ballroom, Eden wrapped herself in the luxurious fox fur and listened to Netty recite Shirley Temple's lines in *Baby Take a Bow*. The veil of sadness had lifted from the little girl, and she laughed in her ermine coat. Grace never took her eyes away from Almond, who sat still as a statue, eyes unblinking. The older girl's black mink pressed against his velvet suit, and she gazed at Almond's handsome face, interlacing her fingers with his.

Eden remembered that moment outside the sitting room when she heard the grief in Grace's voice. The witch had stated that Almond couldn't be raised. Yet here he was, as real as any spirit in Everdark. She had found a way to bring Grace's true love into form.

But something wasn't right about the boy. He hadn't spoken, nor did he seem to recognize Grace, although she didn't seem to mind or was too enraptured to notice. When he locked eyes with Eden, she saw no hint of any personality. Only a deep hollowness and an eternal coldness.

When the movie credits rolled and the film flapped in the projector's wheel, the witch turned on the ballroom lights.

"Love having all my beautiful daughters with me. *Always*."

Grace snuggled against Almond's shoulder, and Netty clapped her hands. The flame of anger reignited in Eden. This wasn't a night of celebration. Not for her. She wasn't the witch's daughter. Eden had been captured, and now she was eternally trapped.

The witch retrieved the fur coats from her daughters. Grace guided Almond out of the ballroom, and Netty skipped behind them. Eden remained at the table, fidgeting with her crinoline slip.

The witch sauntered toward her with a loving smile. "Next time you gon' choose a movie."

"None of the movies I like will be in this place," Eden said.

"That much true," the witch agreed. "But them Spellings got quite a collection. You might find something you fancy."

Eden remained silent. Everything she had once cherished was now gone forever, and she felt the despair deep in her bones.

"Next moonrise, gon' show you something," the witch said. "A special treat, daughter."

The sky was now full of stars. Soon the witch would leave the mansion with her lantern and disappear into the darkness.

"Are you going to take me back to my room now?" Eden asked.

The witch caressed Eden's cheek, her sharp nails softened by a satin glove. "You can find your own way. Nothing can hurt you here. You one of mine now."

CHAPTER TWENTY-NINE
The Mansion at Night

Eden stayed in the north-wing bedroom until she saw the light of the witch's lantern disappear into the Everdark night. Now that she was no longer a prisoner in her room, the crystal doorknob turned effortlessly, and she wandered down the spiral staircase through the library to the great room. Above the fireplace, Renata Spelling sat prim inside the painting, her rotting skin hidden under the dark veil.

"You're trapped here just like me," Eden whispered.

Inspecting the floor, she found no lines of red powder or crushed flowers. No tricks against those with beating hearts. Nothing bright dwelled in the mansion anymore.

Eden started toward the door that led to the lower level of the mansion, but an odd shape loomed on the floor. The dark shadow uncoiled with a thin hiss.

A large black snake with a thick red stripe raised its head, flicking its tongue in warning. Eden slowly retreated as the snake slid in waving motions and coiled itself against the door.

The witch had told Eden that nothing could hurt her in the mansion, but the witch couldn't be trusted. Spirits could be harmed in Everdark. The snake was a message that the lower level was off-limits.

She wandered through the sitting room but stopped at the threshold of the solarium. The glass walls were now dark. After seeing the snake, Eden didn't want to get any closer to the pool. She shivered at the memory of the reptilian croak and the scrape of sharp claws on the porcelain tiles.

Eden moved away and went back into the sitting room. A cracked door piqued her curiosity, but then she heard Grace's faint voice. Eden moved toward the other room and pressed her ear against the closed door to listen. The older girl was speaking to Almond. Eden wondered if Grace was trying to revive his memory.

Panic surged up Eden's neck. Could the dead forget? Who would she be without the memory of who she loved and who had loved her? She took a deep breath to chase the panic away. Netty still remembered her mother. Lorenzo and Isaac still remembered the lives that they had lived. These spirits had retained their memories, but a flake of fear still clung to Eden.

What if I forget? she thought.

Eden moved away from Grace's room and wandered to the south wing of the mansion, passing through the dark kitchen. She advanced up the stairs to a dim hallway decorated with paisley wallpaper. Warm light spilled from an open door, and Eden followed the sound of a blaring trumpet like a welcoming beacon.

She found Bull lounging on his bed. He was no longer the elderly man who served supper, but a young gentleman dressed in dark slacks with a starched shirt layered under a thick sweater. The spirit's socked feet were crossed at the ankles, and his copper-lidded eyes glowed in the lamplight as he read a book. A simple wood desk and chair sparsely decorated the room, and dark green paint adorned the walls. Eden didn't see any of the witch's rot here. In the corner a phonograph played the warbling voice of a woman. Eden cleared her throat, and Bull looked up and gave a broad smile.

"Good evening, Little Eden," he said.

She swallowed a rising lump at the memory of hearing Uncle Willie's musical voice saying her name for the first time on the dock in Marien.

Eden entered the south-wing bedroom and sat at the foot of the bed. "I was looking for Netty. Do you know where she is?"

"Don't know where that child be," Bull answered. "Her room down the hall, but I reckon she would be with you."

Eden stared at the stack of books on Bull's nightstand. "I saw you in the library. Before I . . ." She trailed off, not wanting to say the words.

"When I come here, Miss Mary teach me how to read," Bull said.

"Did you know Mother Mary?" she asked. "From before?"

"Was here long before Miss Mary come to this side, but I knew her people and she knew mine," he answered. "Them Turner women was always brimming with shine."

Eden remembered what the witch had told her. Mary Turner had been born with a caul over her face, a veil full of magic. More gifted than any of her sisters. The witch had been powerful in life, and that power had followed her in death.

"When Mother Mary found you in the cemetery, did you want to go with her?"

"That be what Miss Mary want," Bull answered simply.

Eden wanted to ask if the witch had found him aimlessly wandering the graves. She wanted to know if the witch had saved him or if she had captured him.

"But is that what *you* wanted?" Eden asked again carefully. "Did you want to come here?"

Bull's penny eyes glinted in the lamplight. "Many fine things in Miss Mary's mansion. In my time, them Spellings ain't allow me in the library. Now every book mine."

The song playing on the phonograph ended with scratchy static. Eden wondered if the witch's servant was speaking to her in the same secret language as Netty's, the real meaning in the words not being said.

The trumpet blared again and another song began to play, and Bull nodded his head to the jazzy melody.

"That be Miss Billie Holiday," he said. "Singing 'A Fine Romance' with a white orchestra. Never woulda been possible in my time."

Eden had heard of the singer, known for the signature gardenias that she wore in her hair, but she had never heard this particular song. Eden listened to the lyrics about romantic longing and thought of Grace's love for Almond.

Bull smiled as if lost in a pleasant memory, and Eden felt the familiar safe comfort with him that she had with her great-uncle. But she wanted to ask the spirit so many questions. Why did he look so much younger at night? Did he know about the other trapped spirits? Eden wasn't sure if he would answer her directly or at all.

When the song finished playing, Bull stood up from the bed

and walked to the phonograph. He put the vinyl record back in its sleeve and returned to his perch on the bed, but he didn't pick up his book.

"Need to be careful in the mansion at night," he finally said.

Eden nodded. "There's a snake downstairs."

"You best stay clear. That be Miss Mary's familiar. Got a mighty strong bite."

Eden rose from the bed. "I . . . I should probably go."

"Want me to take you back to your room?" Bull offered.

"No, I'm okay," Eden said. "I promise to be careful."

Bull nestled back onto his pillows and opened his book, his fingers caressing the pages. He seemed content to be here in the mansion as the witch's servant. Maybe the bargain had been this other existence during Everdark night. Young and handsome, Bull now had the eternal freedom to read every book in the Spelling library if he wanted.

Eden left the witch's servant and traveled down the hallway to Netty's room. She peered into the darkness, but the little girl was nowhere to be found.

Eden traveled back down the south-wing stairs and returned to the great room. The black snake was still coiled against the door to the mansion's lower level. But when Eden turned her focus to the fireplace, she gaped at the painting. The dark veil had been lifted and revealed a sunken hole. Renata Spelling was gone.

Eden searched for the ruined spirit with a twitch of alarm, listening for the skeletal scratch of the woman's fingernails against the papered walls. Now that Eden was no longer a bright girl with blood rushing through her veins, Renata Spelling had lost interest, and the former owner of the mansion evaded her.

She gave up her hunt for the ruined spirit and settled on the couch. The wood crackled in the fireplace and glimmered with embers. Eden thought of Lorenzo and Isaac. The brothers were most likely night fishing under Everdark's star-filled sky, the whales and dolphins joyfully greeting them from the depths of the ocean.

A wave of sadness hit Eden, but she quickly wiped away the tears. She wasn't going to dwell in her despair.

Eden ventured back to the sitting room and stood in front of the cracked door. She carefully stepped into the darkness until she found a lamp. The light revealed a large bedroom, gilded in silver with blue damask wallpaper. In the center of the room was a large bed with a satin fabric headboard. The grand wood frame was embellished in a filigreed floral design accented with crystals. All the furniture in the room had the same antique silver finish.

This is the witch's room, Eden thought.

She sat at the gilded vanity, averting her eyes from her indigo reflection. Hairbrushes and marcel irons were neatly placed in a corner of the lacquered table. In the witch's jewelry box, Eden found priceless gems of every shade, strands of pearls, and sparkling bracelets. She leafed through a stack of playbills. Stage shows advertised beautiful showgirls and dashing gentlemen. She stared at a 1924 playbill with the witch on the cover, her dark brown skin luminous in a shimmering white evening gown. She was surrounded by several male admirers, and the front of the program touted the star in red letters: *Mary Turner! Singer, Dancer, Femme Fatale!*

The witch hadn't lied about her life in New York City. She had been famous before the world crashed, and the days of wine and roses ended. Her fortune had fallen, and the witch had returned to Safina Island. A rising star reduced to a maid cleaning a mansion owned by her once adoring fans. This had been the stolen life of Mary Turner.

Eden stood up from the vanity and peeked into the bathroom. Rot traveled down the tiled walls. She moved closer and touched the decay. An oily residue remained on her fingers. She wondered why she was the only spirit to see the blowback in the mansion. Maybe being newly dead had left some of her bright senses untainted by the witch's power.

Surveying the gilded room, Eden felt another surge of sadness. The witch had brought remnants of her life into the spirit world, yet she couldn't truly enjoy them. She had conjured an alternate reality in death, but this powerful feat had done nothing to erase the past and what had been stolen from her.

Eden returned to the north-wing bedroom. Through the open windows, a cool breeze moved through her hair, carrying the salty scent of the ocean. She was an Everdark spirit. Forever bound to this world. The witch's daughter. But this world wasn't real, it was a deception upheld by magic. The witch had twisted its original form, and now the blowback was slowly dissolving it away. Soon everything would rot.

Eden still felt a sharp pang of longing for what she had lost. Her own stolen life. She couldn't return to the world of the living, but maybe she could still change her fate in the world of the dead.

CHAPTER THIRTY
The Witch's Greenhouse

At moonrise, the witch arrived at the north-wing bedroom wearing a simple day dress patterned with a clover design. The witch's hair was in a long, thick braid, reminding Eden of the black snake.

Eden had already changed into the day dress with the mother-of-pearl buttons. She gave the witch a forged smile. "You said you had something to show me. A special treat. What is it?"

The witch pursed her lips in amusement. "You soon see, daughter."

She guided Eden through the glass front doors of the mansion. The moon's bright light covered the grand lawn with a silver sheen. Eden glanced at the grove of orange trees, which were bent heavy with fruit and filled the air with a tangy citrus scent.

They passed the gurgling fountain where the stone angel stood solemnly. Rot crawled up the statue like a devouring disease. Eden paused to stare for a moment before following the witch to the north side of the mansion, toward the greenhouse.

On Uncle Willie's tour of the Renata Mansion, nature had reclaimed the structure, but in Everdark, the greenhouse's sharp angles gleamed under the moon.

The witch opened the door. "I seen how you looked at them flowers in my sitting room."

Eden entered a realm full of plants and blooms. She recognized her mother's favorites. Lily of the valley. Jasmine. Hydrangeas. She touched waxy leaves and velvet petals as the witch collected a tightly woven basket and put on a pair of gardening gloves.

"How does . . . does everything grow here?" Eden asked.

The witch laughed, and the sound bounced against the glass walls. "Moon as bright as the sun."

Eden glanced at the glass ceiling, shading her eyes against the cold glare. A sharp prick of regret hit her. Would she ever see the sun again? She stared at the beautiful flowers that surrounded her. They were vibrant and alive in this dead world.

"Did you plant everything here?"

"Some mine, but them Spellings brung plants from far-off places," the witch replied. "They was always taking things."

She lifted Eden's chin to meet her glowing eyes. Eden stood her ground under the witch's stare, despite knowing sharp nails lay underneath the soft cloth of her gardening gloves. Even though the witch hadn't pushed her into darkness for several moons, Eden was still wary of her power.

"This place make you happy?" The witch's bright eyes glinted in hope.

A lump grew in Eden's throat. In the living world, her mother's summer garden had made her happy. It was full of laughter and love. But after her mother's death, it had also brought Eden sorrow and pain. A bittersweet twist of emotions. Nothing could replace her mother's garden, and she knew the witch's greenhouse could never make her happy.

Eden wasn't Netty. She couldn't dispel the truth of how she

felt. She couldn't bear to use Netty's secret language. When she remained silent, the witch moved away, averting her gaze. But Eden had seen a flash of sadness appear on her beautiful face.

"Take time to get happy," the witch said in a low, soft voice.

Eden wondered if the witch had regrets. She had lavished herself in luxury in a beautiful mansion. She had rescued Netty and given Bull a precious gift. The witch had even raised Grace's true love. Was it so wrong to have the things in death that you had been deprived of in life?

In the witch's silver-gilded bedroom, Eden had seen the stolen life that couldn't be replicated despite the powerful illusion. But she also knew the truth. The witch had betrayed Ruby and held her sister prisoner along with other spirits. She had found Eden on the beach, and instead of escorting her back to the world of the living, the witch let her die and become a bound spirit unable to return. Now the blowback of rot was slowly consuming everything that the witch had created.

Despite her waning magic, the witch still controlled this dark realm. As an Everdark spirit, Eden knew it would be wise to remain on the good side of the witch, and not be the subject of her wrath. If she wanted to change her fate in this spirit world, she needed to earn the witch's trust.

"Before I died, flowers made me very happy," Eden finally said, the secret language flowing off her tongue. "Thank you for showing me your greenhouse, Mother Mary. I may find some happiness here."

The witch flinched in surprise at Eden's words, but then her lips curled into a smile and her eyes flashed with ferocity. "Can be hard adjusting to this world. But you my daughter now. Ain't nothing I won't do to make you happy."

The raw and true emotion unnerved Eden, so she only nodded, unable to speak. *Does the witch truly love me?* she thought.

Mary Turner sauntered down the greenhouse aisles, humming the "Cheek to Cheek" melody as she gathered herbs for her basket. Eden followed the witch from pallet to pallet as she collected thyme, lavender, and rosemary while the moon's cold light shone above them.

They arrived at an aisle full of roses, deep red like blood. Eden bent down to smell one of the blooms, the scent fainter than ones from the living world.

"Roses show us the meaning of balance," the witch stated. "Got beautiful blooms but also thorns. Was always them thorns that interested me. The sharp prick of pain. Remind me of my life."

The witch picked up a pair of sharp scissors and snapped two rose stems, dropping them in her basket. "Renata Spelling ain't allow me in this greenhouse." She frowned, as if speaking it aloud irritated her. "No matter. This greenhouse mine and now yours, too. *Always.*"

Eden stared at the sunflowers leaning against the glass wall. Their yellow blooms reached toward the light of the moon. These flowers were as useful as they were beautiful, because of their seeds. Her mother had always included them in her summer garden.

Now the place that had brought Eden so much joy and pain would be forever lost to her. But here under the pale light of a forever full moon, she was surrounded by everything that her mother had loved.

She was bound to this realm for eternity, and the blooms and the beauty of the witch's greenhouse would never be enough. Eden knew she would never accept this hollow happiness.

CHAPTER THIRTY-ONE

A Packet of Seeds

Eden left the witch in her greenhouse and traveled south to the courtyard, the crashes of waves faint in the distance. Her boots trampled on the seashell path as she walked to the solarium. She gingerly opened the door and stared at the mermaid statue. No traces of rot were on the marble, but Eden noticed a tear on the mermaid's cheek. Eden wondered if the sculptor had put it there by design, knowing such a creature would always yearn for the depths of the ocean.

The solarium was cool and bright, and she inched toward the pool and peered down into the brackish water. Dark shapes lay unmoving at the bottom, as if sleeping. Eden placed her knees on the cool tiles and leaned closer, her hands hovering above the water. What would happen if her fingers broke the surface? Would the creatures wake up and greet her with the sharpness of their teeth? A chill rushed down her spine, and Eden slowly rose from the porcelain tiles.

She left the solarium and walked through the open archway ‹ into the sitting room. Grace and Almond sat on the sofa. The older boy no longer wore the velvet suit but a crisp white shirt that exposed his collarbones and tailored slacks. Grace wore her green-striped day dress and held the boy's hands in hers.

Almond had the same emptiness in his eyes. A shell of a spirit.

"Do you remember when you asked me to dance at the Farmer's Hall? You was shy, but you came over and took my hand. Like this." Grace brought Almond's fingers to her lips, where she pressed a long kiss into his shimmering indigo skin.

Almond only blinked in response, remaining stiff as a mannequin.

"I . . . I don't think he remembers," Eden offered softly.

Grace spun her attention to Eden with glaring eyes. "Don't care what you think. You been dead two moons, what you know about this?"

An apology slid on Eden's tongue, but she held it tight in her mouth. Grace was in denial about Almond. There was something wrong with the spirit. He didn't remember the older girl, and now Eden was certain he never would. His body was here in Everdark, but his spiritual essence hadn't followed him. Eden wondered why the witch would do this to Grace. It seemed worse than never raising the boy at all.

"Do you know where Netty is?" Eden asked, changing from the painful subject of Almond's memory.

"I ain't her keeper," Grace sneered.

Eden knew that she should leave the sitting room and give the young couple their privacy. It was none of her concern. She was newly dead. How did she know how long it took a spirit to remember their life after they were raised? The older girl had been grumpy ever since Eden had known her. Grace wouldn't entertain any theories from a fledging spirit. But then Eden remembered the night when Grace tended her scraped knee.

The older girl had taken care of Eden when she didn't have to do so. But she also remembered Netty's warning. Grace couldn't be trusted. Even so, she would have to learn to coexist with the older girl in the mansion.

"Give him more time," Eden softly said. "I'm sure he'll remember everything."

"Yes," Grace quickly agreed. "Only a matter of time before he remember he love me."

But the emptiness in Almond's eyes only cemented the certainty in Eden's gut. No amount of time, even the eternity of Everdark, would be enough for Almond to remember Grace.

Eden left the sitting room and walked through the great room into the kitchen, where loud clangs and scrapes caught her attention.

She found Bull in his starched servant jacket. He was in front of a cabinet, leaning low to place a flat pan on a lower shelf. His deeply wrinkled hands trembled in effort.

"Let me help you," Eden said.

Bull's copper pennies glinted under the kitchen lights, and he nodded as Eden took the pan and placed it in the cabinet. He was no longer the young gentleman with a book in his hand. Bull was now the witch's elder servant, somber and weak.

"Thank you kindly, Little Eden," Bull said.

She still wanted to ask Bull if the books he took from the library changed him, made him younger. The spirit she saw last night was young enough to be Bull's grandson. But she wasn't sure if the elderly spirit would answer her directly. Inside the mansion, the words that were said had different meanings. If she wanted to get the full answers from Bull, she would have to get him outside the mansion, like Netty had done with her on the beach.

Under the fluorescent lights of the kitchen, she regarded her surroundings. The checkerboard tile gleamed with wax, and the freshly washed white cabinets smelled of bleach. But the walls were flush with rot, pulsing with a decaying heartbeat.

Bull worked solemnly at the kitchen island, separating fresh asparagus and red potatoes into large silver bowls.

"Why do you cook the same thing every night?" she asked.

"That be what Miss Mary want," he answered.

Eden fought against more questions bubbling inside her until finally her curiosity overtook her. "But . . . why even do this? Why does she make you serve us every night? You should be able to sit and eat with us."

Bull's hands hovered and trembled over the bowl of vegetables. Finally he placed them firmly on the kitchen island. "Reckon I should be invited to the table, but that ain't how it work here."

A growing frustration brewed inside Eden. She wasn't sure if any of the spirits would be able to help her. But Eden knew there was something else going in the mansion; a hidden defiance lurked in its walls.

"Nothing will work here when the blowback comes," Eden finally whispered. "Soon everything will be covered in rot."

Bull stopped working and stared at her, the copper pennies bright against his skin. "You seen rot in this house?"

Eden stared at the blighted walls and the spots of decay festering in the corners of the ceiling.

"It's everywhere," she answered. "Even here."

Bull slowly turned away, moving to a cabinet. He tapped open a hidden shelf and pulled out a small envelope.

"I ain't think a bright girl would end up in Miss Mary's mansion. But here you standing before me."

"I'm not bright anymore," Eden corrected him.

"Miss Mary told me you was an empty husk. Shoulda known better to believe her. You still a Gardener girl," the old spirit stated quietly. "And you done seen this world's failing."

Eden looked down at the old man's hands, which were sprinkled with age spots on his starry skin. The small envelope he held was just as frail and worn, yellowing around the edges.

"What's in it?" Eden asked.

"A packet of seeds," he whispered. "Keep them close."

"Do you want me to plant these in the greenhouse?"

"Miss Mary done already took you there?" the old spirit asked.

When Eden nodded, Bull pushed the packet into her hands. "That ain't the place, but you gon' know where to sow them. Keep this on your person and away from Miss Mary."

Eden stood stunned at the way that the old spirit spoke to her now, his voice steady and direct. She put the seeds in the pocket of her day dress. Bull shuffled back to the kitchen island and picked up a paring knife.

"Do you want me to help you with supper?" Eden offered.

"You ain't the help," he answered in a louder tone, returning to his role of witch's servant. "You Miss Mary's daughter. Time for you to leave. You don't belong in this kitchen. Let me make this fine meal on my own."

Eden understood their conversation was now over. The secret language had returned within the walls of the mansion. She touched his shoulder in gratitude.

"I'll keep the seeds close," she whispered. "I promise."

CHAPTER THIRTY-TWO

The Ruined Spirit

When the witch arrived at the north-wing bedroom, Eden used the secret language of the Everdark spirits.

"Mother Mary, will you let me pick out a dress on my own?" Eden asked in a demure voice. "There's so many pretty ones, but I want to choose myself. I want to do my hair, too. Let me surprise you for supper."

The witch beamed in pride. "That would be lovely, daughter. Can't wait to see."

Eden rigged a placid smile on her face that quickly vanished when the witch closed the door.

Earlier, when she had left the kitchen, Eden opened the fragile packet that Bull gave her and found several sunflower seeds of varying colors. Some were as pale as the rising Everdark moon. Others as black as the sand on the beach. A few were speckled, like stars on indigo skin. All the seeds were withered and crusted with dust. She poured them all into a small velvet pouch that had previously held an emerald ring.

As she got ready for supper, Eden pinned the pouch of seeds inside the periwinkle party dress she had chosen, keeping them close just as she had promised Bull that she would. She adorned herself in sapphires and placed opal hairpins in her hair.

Downstairs in the dining room, Eden met the witch's approving gaze with a humble nod and then sat at the dining table next to Netty. She went through the motions of the mansion's loop, eating the eternal meal that Bull had prepared. In the cold ballroom, Eden delighted the witch by choosing *42nd Street* as her movie choice, and then endured the happy music and dancing with a counterfeit smile.

When the loop finished, she returned to the north-wing bedroom and waited at the window until she saw the witch with her lantern disappear into the Everdark night.

Eden crept down the stairs to the great room, where a fire crackled in the hearth. The black snake was coiled in front of the door to the lower level, but she wasn't concerned about its threat. There was only one other spirit she hadn't spoken with in the mansion. A spirit who could offer answers to her questions.

Eden perched on the edge of the couch and stared at the veiled painting above the fireplace mantel. Renata Spelling was in partial shadow, the woman's ruined face plastered with a smile, her hands folded primly in her lap.

"I have nothing but time," Eden spoke aloud to the painting.

But after an hour, Eden stood up and stretched her legs. Closing her eyes, she massaged the tendons in her neck.

A loud ripping sound filled the great room, and Eden opened her eyes. The oil painting revealed a deep gash. Renata Spelling was slowly climbing out of the frame, her skin exposing bone and gristle.

The ruined spirit twisted her torso though the ripped hole in the painting. She grunted as she pushed, her lips pressed into a thin line. Her arms and legs wobbled on the fireplace mantel and then she jumped, her gray mottled feet landing on the floor.

Eden had been holding her breath as she watched Renata Spelling emerge from the painting, but now she forced the air out of her lungs in a frightened swoosh.

The woman brushed bony fingers through her hair, and clumps of her scalp fell to the floor. Eden shuddered as the ruined spirit walked toward her, her exposed teeth and jaw giving her a gruesome smile.

Renata Spelling sat on the couch, and the smell of her mildewed clothes and decaying flesh made Eden cough.

"I remember you," the ruined spirit said in a gravelly voice. "I let you out."

Eden swallowed her fear and found her bravery. "Yes, you did. Why did you do that? Were you trying to help me?"

The woman leaned forward. "I wanted to know what your blood tasted like."

For a moment, Eden felt of rush of panic. Renata Spelling could be as dangerous as the black snake or the plat-eye.

The ruined spirit cackled. "No need to be scared of me, girl. I see Mary's magic on your skin. Such a shame."

Relief spread along Eden's arms, and she relaxed her shoulders to focus on the questions she wanted to ask the former owner of the mansion.

"Why are you in Everdark?" she asked.

Renata Spelling regarded her with a cold hatred. "Everdark? Is that what you people call it now? You think I *want* to be here with *all* of you?"

Eden ignored the vitriol of the woman's words. "How did you get here? Did the witch catch you?"

The ruined spirit closed her eyes and whimpered, as if trying to avoid a bad memory. But when she opened them again, they were full of malice. "Why did you decide to stay? What did she promise you?"

"I . . . I didn't choose to stay," Eden stumbled.

"Another one of her collected pets. Poor thing." Renata Spelling stood up and walked to the fireplace, her morbid silhouette dark against the orange glow.

"Did you curse Charles Spelling to death?" Eden asked.

"Why is that your concern, girl?"

When Eden didn't answer, Renata Spelling turned back to face her. "Death was a mercy to my husband, and it is my wish to join him. I ache for death. But I suffer and live in this house of lies."

"Why are you different from the rest of us?" Eden asked.

"Don't you dare think you're better than me," the ruined spirit spat. "This place is Mary's abomination."

"Shut your mouth," a voice said from the shadows.

Netty moved into the firelight. She was still wearing the pale blue party dress from supper. She glowered at the ruined spirit in bitterness.

"Your fault you here with us," the little girl said. "You know what you done."

Renata Spelling released an angry groan and clutched her bony fingers into fists, but she made no threatening moves toward Netty. As one of the witch's daughters, the little girl was also protected.

"You don't deserve any of this!" the ruined spirit shouted. "This is my house! Charles built it for *me*. Get out!"

"Ain't yours no more," Netty said, calmness in her voice. "This Mother Mary's house now. You best to keep remembering that."

"Mary is lying to you like she lied to me. You'll see. A leopard can't change its spots."

Renata Spelling gathered her moldy gown and pushed her chin in the air. With disdain, she walked away and disappeared into the sitting room. The sound of her bony fingers scratching the walls soon faded as she traveled to the second level of the mansion.

Netty sat next to Eden on the couch. "No need to be scared. She ain't nobody."

"Why did you say it was her fault?" Eden asked. "For being here?"

"She killed Mother Mary with poison," Netty answered.

"What?" Eden gasped, but then she remembered what the witch had told her. *My life was stolen. Did you know that? Just took from me.*

She had thought the witch had meant that her life as a star had been stolen. She didn't know that the witch had been murdered.

"My great-uncle . . . he told me that Renata Spelling laid a trick on her husband."

"Weren't no trick. But she did kill him. She try to get Mother Mary to do it, since she had heard the other servants in the house whispering. Promised Mother Mary a lot of money to do the deed too," Netty continued. "But when Mother Mary refuse, she poison her right along with her husband, then blamed Mother Mary for all of it. Now she getting her own blowback."

Eden stared at the ripped painting. Renata Spelling had betrayed the witch and stolen her life, but that deception had a price. Now she was rotting in Everdark as punishment.

"Mother Mary never wanted to come back to Safina," Eden whispered. "She wanted to be a star."

The witch had brought the darkness of her death upon this world. But she had unleashed her wrath against other spirits, holding them captive and stripping them of their power. It didn't matter that a certain few were showered in her goodness. She had transformed the Renata Mansion into a shrine of her anger and revenge.

Eden was newly dead, but she knew deep in her bones that she couldn't endure this spirit world. Not with the witch's blow-back looming. In this afterlife, she was going to have to find a way to destroy the witch's domain.

She squeezed Netty's hand. "Do you remember the sun?"

"Yes," the little girl answered. "I remember."

CHAPTER THIRTY-THREE

Memories of the Sun

Eden and Netty ventured through the mansion's glass doors into the night. Starlight shimmered in the sky, and Eden's eyes adjusted to the darkness.

They stood on the vast grand lawn, blades of grass soft beneath their shiny buckled shoes. Gurgling water from the fountain offered a peaceful sound in the nocturnal quiet. Without the moon, the tabby walls of the witch's mansion were muted in the gloom and windows reflected shadows.

The last time Eden had been here, she was ravaged with fever and betrayed by Ruby. Her last hope of returning to the world of the living yanked away. Now she was a child of Everdark, and the memory of her demise bubbled up with anger to the surface of her indigo skin.

She guided Netty in front of the marble angel. The little girl glanced back at the mansion's dim portico and moved closer to the fountain, her luminous eyes glowing in the Everdark night.

"Do you see the blowback on the angel?" Eden asked.

Netty stared at the statue, and Eden waited to see if the spirit would see the cracks of decay that disfigured the angel into a morbid relic. After a few moments, the little girl shook her head.

"Don't see nothing," Netty said.

"I can see it. Mother Mary's magic is growing weaker," Eden said. "There's rot even in her room. How much longer do we have?"

"Don't know," Netty whispered. "Reckon not long."

"I want to show you something." Eden reached inside her party dress and unpinned the velvet pouch.

Netty peered at the seeds in Eden's hand. "Who gave them seeds to you?"

"Bull," Eden answered. "He told me I would know where to sow them."

"We best go to the greenhouse," she said.

"Bull said that wasn't the place," Eden said. "And I . . . I don't want to go back there."

"Mother Mary done took you there already?" Netty asked.

"She thought it would make me happy." Eden's voice cracked.

"I reckon it ain't do that."

Eden had lied to the witch, but she couldn't lie to Netty. The greenhouse only intensified the grief of what she had lost. A reminder of what she would never have again.

Netty fidgeted with the taffeta sleeve of her party dress. "I didn't know Bull had them seeds, but we need to go to the greenhouse while Mother Mary ain't here."

"I don't understand," Eden said.

"Need to see if you got the Gardener gift." She grabbed Eden's hand, pulling her toward the greenhouse.

But Eden resisted. "I don't have any magic, Netty!"

The little girl let go of her hand. Eden met her gaze and

saw wisdom that spanned time and generations. In this moment, Netty wasn't childlike at all.

"I seen you in my dreams," she whispered. "Crossing over into this world take power. Nobody seen it here in this world yet. Not Mother Mary. Not even you. But to me, you full of magic."

"There was an elder in Willow Hammock. Miss Nadine," she whispered. "She could see the shine on my skin."

The little girl's dark face erupted in a faint grin, a confident knowing. She offered her hand, and Eden reluctantly took it.

She followed Netty into the greenhouse, the place that would prove her power. She wasn't sure what was supposed to happen or what was waiting for her humming in the soil.

Bright starlight filtered through the glass roof, but darkness still loomed over the plants and sleeping flowers. Netty passed long pallets of herbs, touching the leaves with her small fingers. Earlier, the witch had filled her basket with herbs. Eden thought of the blood-red roses and their sharp thorns.

"When Mother Mary first brung you here, you ain't feel nothing?" Netty asked.

"I only felt sad," Eden answered.

The little girl hesitated and frowned. "You ain't feel no tingle in your fingers? No itch?"

Eden shook her head, and Netty mumbled to herself as she rambled to the back of the greenhouse and stood in front of the row of sunflowers. The tall, wide stems reached outward, blooms facing upward to the glass roof.

"Bull gave you them seeds after you left here," Netty said. "We gon' see what happens now."

Eden scrunched her face in confusion as the little girl pushed her in front of the sunflowers.

"Hold still," Netty said. "Let them get a good look at you."

"What? This doesn't make—" Eden froze as one of the sunflowers leaned down, the bloom staring at her with its brown eye.

Soon the rest of the sunflowers followed suit, their yellow petals inspecting her face and hair. They nestled closer, and Eden slowly touched one of the blooms.

A wisp of bright green light flowed from her fingers, and the flower's wide leaf wrapped around her wrist. Eden exhaled in wonder.

Netty clapped, giddy with excitement. "Them flowers seen your shine."

The sunflowers embraced her fully, devouring her green light. They inched taller and their stems grew thicker. The seeds in the velvet pouch pulsed like tiny heartbeats against her chest. When the light from her fingers faded, the sunflowers moved away and sighed in contentment. Their stalks bent back upright, and the blooms raised their eyes back up to the star-filled sky.

Eden had seen this power on the boat with Isaac. The little boy had manifested deep-blue light into this world. The ocean had known him, and now the sunflowers knew her.

Other plants and flowers in the greenhouse sprang to life. They wiggled leaves and opened their petals. Vines unfurled and reached for her ankles. The sunflowers had awakened their memory of a kindred spirit. A Gardener girl was in their midst.

Netty's eyes glowed in determination. The wisdom and fierceness of generations returned to the little girl's face.

"You ain't no empty husk, but we best be careful now," she said. "We can't let Mother Mary know about this."

"What are we going to do?" Eden asked.

"Mother Mary always go out at night," Netty said. "Next time Mother Mary leave with her lantern, we gon' meet in the orange grove."

CHAPTER THIRTY-FOUR
Secrets of the Grove

Eden stood in front of the open windows, peeling an orange from a basket on her nightstand. She had finished eating the last slice when she spotted the witch's lantern flickering in the darkness.

Earlier that evening, when the mansion's loop finished, she had returned to the north-wing bedroom and taken off her party dress. Now she wore a high-necked blouse and skirt with boots. She was ready to go meet Netty in the orange grove.

Eden traveled down the spiral stairs into the library and found Bull standing in front of a bookcase. The witch's servant was dressed in black slacks and a tan cardigan, his face unlined and young. His penny-lidded eyes glinted in the low light as he gave her a nod.

"Find something good to read?" she asked.

"Revisiting my favorites," Bull answered, patting the spines of two books in his hands.

Eden still wanted to ask him why he was younger during the Everdark night. Curiosity bubbled in her chest, but she ignored it. Netty was waiting.

"Maybe one night you can read to me," she said.

"Pleasure be all mine," Bull paused. "You keeping them seeds close?"

Eden touched the pouch of seeds pinned under her blouse. "Yes."

"You and Netty be careful now," he said.

Eden swallowed and nodded. Did Bull know about the meeting in the orange grove? Her curiosity bubbled up again, but she waved her farewell and left the library.

In the great room, the red-striped snake and Renata Spelling were in their respective places. She gave them wary glances before opening the mansion's front doors.

Her boots crunched on the seashell path as she made her way to the grove. Eden ducked under branches bent heavy with fruit. Netty was waiting for her in an open space between the trees. She had changed into her pink-striped day dress but was still wearing diamond earrings from supper.

"Grace ain't seen you?" Netty asked.

"I—I don't think so," Eden stuttered, because she had forgotten about the older girl, although she was confident Grace was in her room with Almond. "I saw Bull in the library. He told us to be careful."

"Bull on our side," Netty said. "He gave you them seeds."

Eden followed Netty as she strode deeper into the grove until they met another spirit, who waited for them underneath a tree. When Ruby rose from the ground, Eden plucked an unripe orange and threw it at the young girl.

Netty rushed between them. "Don't be cross with Ruby."

"She's a liar!" Eden shouted, rage spilling from her mouth. "She's the reason I'm still here."

"Be quiet now," Netty warned. "Don't need nobody hearing us."

Eden scowled in anger. If she had known that Ruby would be in the orange grove, she would have never agreed to come. The young girl had betrayed her. There wasn't anything Ruby could say to her now.

"Is this why you brought me here?" Eden asked bitterly. "To meet with her?"

"Please listen," Ruby pleaded.

"Don't talk to me," Eden snapped.

Did Netty want them to be friends? Eden may be trapped in Everdark, but she wasn't going to forgive Ruby. It would be a grudge she would keep for eternity. Netty touched Eden's shoulders, but she tugged away from the little girl's grasp. She sulked, but then finally gazed into Netty's eyes. They beamed again with the same fierceness she had seen in the greenhouse, a wisdom that spanned multiple lifetimes.

"Last moon you ask me about the sun," Netty said quietly. "Well, Ruby remember the sun too."

Eden glared at the young girl, but her anger softened as tears glazed in Ruby's eyes and a fat drop trailed down her cheek.

"You got power in you," Netty continued. "You ain't no empty husk. Them plants seen you. Things ain't getting no better. Soon Mother Mary's blowback gon' overcome this world."

Eden knew it was true. The witch's magic was failing. Everything in Everdark would eventually decay and crumble. This spirit world couldn't continue to exist with only the pain of thorns.

She regarded the two spirits in the orange grove. They had polar relationships with the witch. Ruby was a known enemy, but

Netty was a favorite daughter. Now these opposite forces had come together for a common cause and wanted her to join them.

"Mother Mary has to be stopped," Ruby said. "Bad things gon' happen if we don't do something. If we get her gone, the sun can come back and Old Buzzard will leave us be."

"You ain't got to stay," Netty added. "You can move on and find your mama."

Eden had stopped scratching marks for moonrises when she became an Everdark spirit. She didn't know if her father was still searching for her or if he was weeping alone with the tragic loss. Eden knew that she could never return to him, but if she were able to move on from this spirit world, she could be reunited with her mother.

If they defeated the witch, she would no longer be stuck in a dark in-between, no longer bound to Everdark for eternity. Netty's words held this hope, but just as quickly doubt snuffed their possibility.

"The witch is too powerful," Eden finally whispered. "I'm not strong enough to defeat her."

"You ain't the only one with a gift. Remember Isaac, who brung you to the house with his brother?" Ruby asked.

Eden nodded. "I saw his power with the ocean, but I still don't think it's enough to stop the witch."

Netty furrowed her brow in silent agreement, but Ruby's face held stern and fierce.

"Lorenzo ain't convinced either," the young girl said. "Mainly he don't want Mother Mary finding out about Isaac, but if I tell him about you then he might change his mind."

Eden touched the pouch of seeds through her blouse. "I'm not sure what I even can do."

"A Gardener girl can do plenty," Netty said.

"I . . . I don't know." Eden stumbled over her words. She hated the doubt in her cold heart. Hadn't she been determined to find a way to destroy the witch's domain? Why did she feel this fear of failure? She knew the witch had to be stopped.

Eden was full of magic, but she was also scared. She didn't know how to use her power. How could her gift stand up against the witch who had conquered an entire world?

The leaves rustled and trembled above them. After a few tense moments, an Everdark bird fluttered into the sky.

"Best be leaving now." Netty turned to Ruby. "Give my sister a moon to think about it."

The young girl wrapped her shawl tight around her. "That seem fair. Come to the house. I can send for Lorenzo and Isaac."

"You head out first," Netty told Eden. "Be making my way back to the mansion after a spell."

Ruby and Netty disappeared into the grove's shadows. Eden still wasn't sure she trusted Ruby, but the young girl was willing to help her to destroy Everdark. Even with her betrayal, they still had a common enemy.

When Eden returned to the mansion's portico, Grace opened the front doors, a frown plastered on her face. "I seen you leave, where you been?"

Eden glimpsed at the orange grove. Night shrouded the trees. Netty and Ruby were gone, hidden and safe.

"I . . . I saw a black cat and tried to follow it," Eden blurted out. "But I lost it."

The older girl narrowed her eyes. "You best stay away from that black cat. Mother Mary been hunting for that wretch."

Eden hadn't seen the black cat since its appearance in the woods, and the mysterious creature hadn't returned to the mansion since her death. But Eden knew there was nothing the black cat could do to help her now.

"Thanks for the warning." Eden avoided Grace's glare as she slid past her into the mansion.

CHAPTER THIRTY-FIVE
The Witch's Lantern

I n the bright light of the Everdark moon, Eden played the role of the witch's daughter. She used the secret language and averted her eyes from the expanding rot on the mansion's walls.

At supper and in the ballroom, Grace watched Eden with a steady gaze. Almond's memory still hadn't returned and he remained a shell of a spirit, but the older girl had changed her focus from the boy she loved to her eternal sister. Eden knew she had to be very careful around the witch's spy.

Although her Gardener gift had been awakened, the seeds stayed dormant in the velvet pouch beneath Eden's clothes. Tiny heartbeats didn't flutter against her chest. Eden had stared at her shimmering indigo fingers, willing for the Gardener magic to flow through them, but nothing happened. She wasn't sure how her magic worked. Isaac seemed to call his gift forth when his hands were in the ocean. Maybe it was similar for her with plants and flowers. But Netty had warned Eden that the witch couldn't find out about her new power, so she steered clear of the greenhouse.

Now she lay on the bed in the north-wing bedroom. She had endured another version of the mansion's loop. Eden's decision loomed as the moon set behind the trees. She wasn't sure if her fledging gift was any match against the witch's power, but now every wall in the mansion was fully covered with rot, and Eden knew that she had no choice but to try.

She sneaked out of the mansion, passing through the dark solarium, and waited in the shadows of the courtyard. Grace's door had been closed, but Eden didn't want to take any chances this time. When the older girl didn't emerge from her room, Eden made her way down to the black beach. Netty had told her that they could no longer meet in the orange grove.

The waves swooshed calmly against the shore as she stared out to the dark horizon. Eden's boots trudged on the sand toward the woods. It was the same path where she had run for her life, Netty's screams haunting her. She shuddered at the memory, which now felt like a lost dark dream.

The woods enveloped her, but Eden didn't fear the creature calls of the night. She searched for Netty's mark, pink ribbons on branches, and tracked the spirit's path. The little girl had told her that she would signal the way to the house covered in frost. Now, with three satin ribbons in her grip, she traveled down a steep bank near a river. Silent on the soft ground, her boots sank in the mud.

Two goldenrod eyes blinked at her in the gloom. Eden gasped at the swish of a fluffy tail. She held the black cat's gaze as it moved closer to her. The creature seemed larger than Eden remembered. A faint sadness bloomed on her skin.

"Seems like we found each other too late," she whispered.

The black cat sat in front of her for a moment, as if agreeing with her statement, but then it prowled away, looking back as if it wanted her to follow.

Eden hesitated. The other spirits were waiting for her at the frost house. She needed to stay on Netty's path, but she wanted to see where the black cat would lead her. Would it be able to return Eden to the world of the living if she followed? Would the black cat bring her to a jagged opening of sunshine? Would she see Aunt Susanna's mint-green house? No, it was too late for her to return to Willow Hammock. But Eden couldn't deny her strong curiosity and veered off her path.

Starlight filtered through the trees as Eden ventured deeper into the woods, keeping her eye on the black cat. Eden's skin buzzed with anticipation.

They arrived at a clearing. Dead trees surrounded a small, blighted shack with a sagging tin roof. Nothing dwelled near and the shack leaned dangerously on rotting stilts. The crumbling steps led to a front porch where a lantern glowed in the darkness. When the door opened, Eden quickly hid behind the massive trunk of a live oak, Spanish moss tickling her neck.

The witch appeared on the porch. Her hair was loose, and stretched coils settled on her shoulders. She wore her night-walking clothes, a high-necked blouse with a long skirt. The witch walked down the steps of the shack but stopped and examined the dark sky.

A large bird swooped low, but the witch didn't cower. When the creature landed in the yard, Eden realized it was Old Buzzard, the god-spirit who Ruby had met in the road. A tiny shiver crept up Eden's spine.

He stalked toward the witch, sharp claws scarring the dirt and eyes gleaming with malice. The witch finally bowed low, dropping to her knees, while the god-spirit considered this action. Old Buzzard pressed his large claw on the witch's head and pushed her face into the dirt.

"Answer still no." The witch's voice was muffled but defiant.

The buzzard bellowed in anger but lifted his massive claw. The witch slowly rose from the dirt, her chin held high.

"Ain't nothing changed," she said. "You can't have none of them other spirits neither. They mine too. Everything here mine. Now leave me be. My sisters coming and you best not be here when they arrive."

Despite the witch's warning, the buzzard didn't move. Mary Turner stood her ground and glowered at the god-spirit in an unsettling standoff. But after a few moments, she turned away and strolled to the porch, picking up her lantern.

"We done here," she said.

Old Buzzard cawed again before spreading his large wings and taking off. Wiping dirt from her face, the witch stared at the night sky. After taking one last look at the ruined shack, she disappeared into the woods.

Eden let out a slow shaking breath. Old Buzzard was waiting on the witch to accept his offer. Mary Turner was rejecting him now, but the blowback was coming and would tarnish every beautiful thing the witch had conjured. The rot of her stolen magic would be the only thing left. Would she be tempted to accept an offer to return Everdark back to its previous glory?

Eden searched around for the black cat, but it was gone.

She also realized that she had dropped Netty's ribbons and was off the path to the frost house. Eden glanced back at the ruined shack, and curiosity rumbled in her bones.

She moved from her hiding place and tiptoed into the barren yard, searching the star-filled sky for Old Buzzard. After a few moments, she slowly traveled up the steps and entered the shack.

There was no furniture or stove in the large room, but a quilt lay in the east corner covered with sepia-colored photographs. Eden leaned closer to inspect them. Portraits of beautiful women in cotton and lace dresses. Eden counted six of them. In another photograph, there was a family portrait with the same six women posed around a little girl. They stood in front of a small house with a tin roof. A snapshot from the past. Powerful women who were now long gone.

"Mother Mary's sisters," Eden whispered.

Beside the quilt lay a basket of rotten oranges and decaying herbs. Melted wax from black and red candles surrounded them. Two long-stemmed roses had been placed on the quilt, but now they were withered and dead, with sharp thorns.

Eden returned her focus to the quilt, lingering on the pictures of the women. This was the witch's lineage. She had told Old Buzzard they were coming.

"Why you here in the Turner house?" a voice asked behind her.

Eden yelped and turned to a dark silhouette in starlight. Netty moved from the front door and into the shack, a fistful of ribbons in her hand.

"Worried you was lost," the little girl said.

"Mother Mary was here. What was she doing?" Eden asked.

"She calling to her sisters for help," Netty answered.

"How long has she been coming here?"

Netty stood beside Eden and stared down at the pictures of the Turner women, a frown on her face. "Long before she found me."

Eden swallowed. "They're not coming back, are they?"

The little girl shook her head. "They done forsaken her."

"Old Buzzard was also here," Eden said. "Mother Mary didn't take his offer."

Netty eyes filled with alarm. "She been leaving him be for now, but one night she gon' take him up on his offer. He smell this dying world. Reason why he came here in the first place. Only a matter of time."

Eden knew the only way to keep this world away from the god-spirit was to defeat the witch.

"We should go meet the others," Eden finally said.

CHAPTER THIRTY-SIX

A Reunion of Spirits

The eternal sisters hiked into the woods to the house covered in frost. Squirrels followed them as they continued their journey, springing noisily from branch to branch. Eden stayed vigilant for any appearance from the black cat. She wondered why the creature had led her to the Turner house. What had been its purpose? Did the black cat want Eden to see the witch with Old Buzzard?

Eden stopped when a hulking figure emerged from a cluster of resurrection ferns. The plat-eye's red eyes glowed in the darkness, but the monster dog didn't growl or reveal its sharp teeth. Instead the Everdark creature greeted Netty happily and wagged its tail.

The little girl scratched between the plat-eye's pointy ears. "You ain't bright no more, so he won't bite you."

Eden cowered from the monster dog. "That's not going to make me pet him."

The plat-eye rolled on the ground like a puppy while Netty cooed and rubbed his belly. Satisfied with the attention, the Everdark creature rebounded on its legs and gave a joyful bark before trotting away into the night. Despite observing the plat-eye being docile and playful, Eden still trembled when it howled in the distance.

They left the woods and traveled down a wide dirt road. The tall white steeple of First Church sprouted above the tree line. Eden remembered the Gardener family celebration and the ring shout performed by her relatives. The singing voices and clapping hands. If they defeated the witch, maybe that kind of joy could return to these spirits.

Eden and Netty trekked across a field to the frost house, which shimmered in the starlight. Ruby greeted them at the door. She was wrapped in a shawl, her head covered with a white head wrap.

"You found her," she said.

Lorenzo and Isaac were sitting in front of the wood-burning stove. The older brother stood up first, and Eden gave him a weak smile.

"Ruby told us what happened." Lorenzo paused to glare at her. "Don't like it, but what's done been done."

Isaac moved forward and took Eden's arm. The little boy examined her hand closely, staring at the glimmer in her indigo skin. "You one of us now."

"It's not your fault," Eden told him.

Ruby poured Netty a cup of tea, and Eden accepted one as well. The brew had the same clean taste as when she had sipped it as a bright girl with a beating heart. Eden's anger at the young girl's betrayal was still fresh, but if she wanted to defeat the witch, she knew that she would have to swallow her bitter feelings.

"Told the brothers you ain't no empty husk," Ruby said.

Isaac's glowing eyes shifted to her. "What can you do?"

"I'm not quite sure," Eden admitted. "But the plants know me like the ocean knows you."

"Not everybody get the shine," Netty said. "My mama was full of it. But I was born empty."

"I ain't got none neither. Ade got all the shine," Ruby said.

"And you seen what happened to her." Lorenzo frowned. "Mother Mary got ahold of it."

"That's why we have to put her down before she find out about us," Isaac said, his eyes full of bravery.

The older boy shook his head, unconvinced. "She too powerful from what she done took from Ruby's sister and them other elders."

"You right to be concerned, but we got to try. We can't wait for the blowback. Y'all know it coming," Netty said.

"What gon' happen if we fail?" Lorenzo pushed the question in front of them, his eyes steady with concern.

"Failing ain't a part of this," Ruby said.

Lorenzo rubbed his face in worry. "Isaac and Eden gon' be empty husks when Mother Mary get done with them."

"Blowback still coming," Netty repeated. "We got to do something."

"I saw Mother Mary tonight," Eden told them. "Old Buzzard came to her."

The other spirits' eyes all focused on Eden. Netty nodded to confirm it was true. Ruby adjusted her shawl as if she were cold, and Isaac moved closer to the wood-burning stove. Just the mention of the god-spirit put a shiver in the room.

"She didn't take his offer." Eden paused. "She thinks her sisters are coming."

"They ain't coming," Ruby said. "Old Buzzard know that too.

He just gon' bide his time until this world rot. When the blow-back finally take over, he know Mother Mary gon' accept his offer."

Netty touched Eden's hand. "When she take his offer then he gon' take us all away to do his bidding against bright folks. Haunting and harming souls. We be bound to him for eternity."

"But I thought . . . don't we have to accept his offer too?" Eden was confused.

"We can if we want," Ruby said. "He would take us. But this Mother Mary's world and her magic on our skin. She take his offer, everything she done touched go to him."

Eden had thought that only Everdark itself would be under the god-spirit's domain. She hadn't known that she could be used as a harmful spirit against the living, possibly haunting the ones she loved. It was a greater danger than the witch's blowback.

Lorenzo retreated to the small window next to the door, and Eden joined him. The older boy gazed outside at the darkened field, his face somber and sad.

The risk was great. The only hope was five children fight-ing against a powerful witch. If they failed, the blowback would destroy Everdark and drown them in eternal rot. But even worse, if the witch took the buzzard's offer, they would all be in deeper peril.

"The odds may be against us, but we don't have a choice," Eden said. "You don't want Old Buzzard taking us away. I know you don't want that for Isaac. Or me. Any of us."

Lorenzo's glowing eyes were full of struggle. He wanted to protect his brother from the witch's harm, but there was a larger danger looming over all of them.

Eden grasped the older boy's hand, and they returned to the other spirits. Lorenzo took a moment to regard each of them before he spoke.

"Eden and Isaac need to work. Get stronger in they gifts," he finally said.

"Far from Mother Mary's eyes," Ruby quickly agreed. "Pirate Island be the best place for Eden and Isaac to work."

"They can go to the south side of the island near the old fort," Lorenzo said. "Mother Mary never come that way."

"How much time will we need?" Eden asked.

"I ain't quite sure," Ruby answered. "But the sooner y'all start, the better."

The children of Everdark gathered in front of the wood-burning stove. The powers of the ocean would be intertwined with gifts of the garden. Eden still had no idea how her magic worked, but she was willing to try and figure it out. Their combined magic would have to be enough to defeat the witch.

"Let's start next moon," Eden said.

CHAPTER THIRTY-SEVEN

No Sisters Here

The stars were fading into Everdark twilight, waiting for the moon to rise. Eden and Netty passed under the low-hanging branches of the orange grove, making their way back to the mansion.

"You first," the little girl said. "Then after a spell gon' follow you."

Eden moved forward but then suddenly stopped. The witch's lantern flickered on the mansion's portico and a cold dread crawled over her skin.

"What you see?" Netty whispered from behind her.

Eden scurried back into the darkness of the orange grove. "Mother Mary is back before the moonrise."

"We can't hide now," the little girl answered.

Netty gripped Eden's hand, guiding them to the grand lawn. The mansion doors opened, and the witch appeared in her night-walking clothes, but now the black snake was coiled around her neck like a morbid necklace.

"Been looking for y'all," the witch said.

Netty skipped up the mansion's stairs, childlike and innocent. "Took my sister to the beach. We been hunting shells."

The witch caressed Netty's cheek, and the snake lifted its

head, flicking out a forked tongue. The red stripe glistened on its black skin.

"You found any?" the witch asked. "Show me."

Netty faltered but quickly regained her composure. "We ain't found none good for collecting. Maybe next time."

Grace sauntered onto the portico wearing her green-striped day dress. Instead of a frown, the older girl had a cruel smile on her face.

Something's wrong, Eden thought. *Something's changed.*

"Netty, I don't fancy lying," the witch said.

The little girl laughed, a bright cheerful sound in the dark. "I ain't never lie to you, Mother Mary."

"Stop playacting like you in a movie," Grace finally said. "We know where you been. What you been doing."

Netty stayed silent, and Eden swallowed a cold lump of fright. The witch sighed, as if catching Netty in a lie was a mere inconvenience.

"When Grace told me you been gallivanting with Ruby, I knew she had to be mistaken, because my daughter would never do such a thing," the witch said.

"You know Ruby hate us," the older girl said. "She wanna destroy everything we got."

Netty jutted out her chin and sneered at Grace. "You ain't my sister. I only got one sister who love me."

Grace let out a shrewd laugh. "Ain't no sisters here, Netty."

The witch grabbed Netty's arm, pulling her close. "No more fooling me now. You been with Ruby?"

"I done told you already." The little girl's voice was weak. "We was at the beach."

The witch released Netty and her eyes turned pitch-black. Pushing her hands up to the night sky, the witch churned the wind. Strong gusts whipped through Eden's hair and clothes. Netty ascended, and her boots dangled in the empty air. The little girl clutched at her neck. The witch regarded Netty as she struggled to breathe with disdain and disappointment.

"Stop! You're hurting her!" Eden finally shouted.

The witch drew her black eyes to Eden. Netty dropped to the portico's floor and crawled away, gasping for breath.

"Don't think I ain't gon' deal with you." The witch tramped down the mansion stairs to the grand lawn. "I seen you spying on me behind that tree."

Eden wanted to run, but she couldn't leave Netty. She straightened and stood firm, courage seeping into her bones. A flurry of wind blew the witch's hair up in a torrent of cottony waves. She was beautiful in the gloom, her liquid black eyes deep and dangerous.

"You don't own this world!" Eden found the bravery to speak.

The witch marched toward her. "I *made* this world, daughter."

"You didn't make it." Eden's voice cracked with fright. "You stole it like you stole me!"

The witch raised her hands again, forcing Eden in the air. A coldness entered her body, bleak and sharp.

"You forget yourself," the witch said. "You are *mine*. Everything here mine."

Eden fought to breathe and struggled to keep pure terror from enveloping her. Wisps of black smoke unfurled from the witch's long, sharp nails and surrounded her, smothering Eden in murky shadows.

The pouch of seeds fluttered to life, hammering against Eden's chest. Tiny heartbeats of resistance. Eden closed her eyes and the sunflowers appeared bright behind her lids, and a surging power flowed within her body. Pinpricks of light escaped through her skin, the color of fresh leaves.

Swirling in gradients of green, Eden's power burst through the witch's shroud of smoke and surrounded Eden in a radiant aura, sheltering her against the dark.

The witch gasped, and the oily blackness dissolved from her eyes. Released from the spell, Eden fell hard on the lawn, a sharp pain piercing her knees.

The witch towered over her. "You been keeping secrets from me, daughter."

Eden heard the words as if she were enclosed in a glass case. When the witch's eyes turned black again, Eden quickly pushed her hands out in defense, hurling an arrow of light. The witch chuckled as it evaporated in the dark shroud of her magic. Eden's gift was still weak, and not a match for the powerful Witch of Everdark. The seeds stuttered, and fear broke out on Eden's skin in a cold sweat.

The black snake unfurled from the witch's neck. It slid quickly over the grass and loomed over Eden, its red stripe glowing in the dark storm of the witch's magic.

"Seem you ain't no empty husk after all," the witch said. "But you soon will be."

The snake opened its mouth full of fangs. Eden shrieked

in pain as it bit into her shoulder. The green glow around her dulled, seeping away as the snake greedily devoured it.

Eden tussled with the snake. She tried to resist, but the witch's magic was too strong. The heartbeats of the seeds grew weaker, pulsing slower until they finally stopped and the last ember of light faded. The snake pulled its fangs from her shoulder, its red stripe now green and full of Eden's magic. The seeds were now dormant, unmoving against her chest. She was empty, her Gardener gift stolen.

Netty's screams were the last thing Eden heard before she fell into darkness.

CHAPTER THIRTY-EIGHT

Elder Spirits

A dull pain throbbed at the back of Eden's head, and her throat felt scratchy, as if she was on the verge of getting sick with a cold. She had awakened in someone's lap. A calloused hand caressed her cheek.

"Everything gon' be all right," a voice above her said.

The woman's hair was covered with a white head wrap. Eden's keen eyes surveyed her surroundings. A handful of other spirits watched them in the gloom.

"She 'wake?"

Eden tried to sit up at the sound of Netty's voice, but the woman gently stopped her. "No need for moving."

"Where am I?" she asked.

"Bottom of the mansion," Netty answered. "Mother Mary and Grace brung us down here."

Eden slumped in the unknown spirit's lap. She was trapped behind a locked door again. "How long has it been?"

"Ain't no time in Everdark," the woman answered.

"Mother Mary took my gift from me," Eden sputtered, her voice cracking in sorrow.

The woman's rough hands wiped away Eden's tears. "That ain't none of your fault."

"She was hurting Netty. I tried to fight her, but I wasn't strong enough yet."

"Don't fret on that. Nobody fault but mine," Netty said quietly. "Shoulda been more careful."

The other spirits slunk closer. They were old and weak, drained of their gifts. None had any power in the lower levels of the mansion. Not anymore.

"Who are you?" Eden asked the woman.

"My name Ade," the spirit answered.

"I met your sister," Eden said. "She's been trying to get you out of here."

"Ruby got a stubborn mind."

"Your sister is stubborn . . . and brave," Eden said.

A touch of pride set on Ade's face as Eden slowly unfolded her limbs. She was still in the day dress with the mother-of-pearl buttons and wearing her boots. A dirt floor was beneath her, damp and cold.

Ade and Netty propped Eden against a wall. She inspected the other spirits in the room. They had stooped backs and wrinkled faces filled with misery.

Netty crouched beside her. "Sorry, sister."

"Remember what you told me," Eden said. "Sorry doesn't mean anything here."

The little girl stayed quiet as Ade settled in front of them. Her eyes had a sickly yellow tint but were brighter than the other spirits'. How long would it take for Eden's eyes to dim in the sorrowful gloom, forgotten and lost?

"Netty said you was a Gardener," Ade said. "Come here as a bright girl."

"I was in Willow Hammock when I found my way here in the woods." Eden paused. "I was following a black cat but lost it. Then I saw a sliver of night and peeked through. Didn't know I would be trapped here."

There was a shuffling among the other spirits. Weak whispers in the dark. They leaned closer to listen.

"You saw a black cat?" Ade asked. "You seen her since you been here?"

Eden remembered Aunt Susanna's island stories. *Folks even say black cats are godlike themselves and can travel between worlds.* Was the black cat a god-spirit like Old Buzzard?

"I've seen her. She tried to warn me when Ruby . . ." Eden didn't want to tell Ade about her sister's betrayal. "But when I finally found her again, it was too late for me."

"That black cat don't come here often, but you the spitting image of your mama," Ade stated. "Maybe she thought you was Nora Gardener."

"My mom drew this world. That's how I found out about Everdark. I didn't think it was real at first . . . but now . . ." Eden's voice trailed off.

"I first seen your mama in my dreams," Ade said. "Told her what was happening. But when she come here, that plat-eye got ahold of her and there was nothing I could do but send her back."

Eden now understood what had happened. Her mother's terrible accident. Ade had pushed Nora Gardener back into the world of the living. Her mother never got a chance to free these spirits.

"You did a good thing," Eden said. "You saved her life."

The woman bowed her head, heavy with the haunting memory. When she locked eyes with Eden again, there was a shift in Ade's face, a tiny spark of moxie. It reminded Eden of Ruby.

"Since Mary been here, dark been rising," she said. "We done what we could to fight her when she first come here, but Mary is a Turner woman. She was mighty powerful in life. More so in death. Ain't no one here to best her."

"Do you think she'll take Old Buzzard's offer?" Eden asked.

"She got your Gardener gift now. She won't be minding him much," Ade answered. "But her blowback still coming."

Eden's gift had been fledging and weak. She wasn't sure how much power it gave the witch. How much time did they have?

"There has to be a way to get out of here. Can we send a message to Ruby?" Eden asked.

Ade shook her head. "Ain't talked to or seen Ruby since Mary put me down here."

The elder spirits had drifted closer. One of them shifted forward and finally spoke, the voice wisp and faint.

"My name Ophelie. Gardeners gave me a plot of land when them Spellings left. Honor to see one again."

The old woman had kind eyes. Eden reached out and touched her wrinkled hands in gratitude. The elder spirit reminded her of Miss Nadine. Someone who would sit and tell island stories, sharing the culture of their ancestors.

Other spirits came forward with stories of the Gardeners helping them in life. The family had healed their land, helped their crops grow, and given them shelter after emancipation.

Safina Island had been a place of sanctuary, and Willow Hammock had been their home.

Eden pressed her hands to her chest. The pouch of seeds was still pinned underneath her dress. They were fallow now, their pulses of life stolen. But the elder stories gave Eden a glimmer of hope, a small kindling of faith.

She pulled the velvet pouch out of her dress and opened the contents, spilling the seeds into her hand. They were now bleached white, a stark contrast in the gloom. Ade widened her eyes.

"Your mama gave me those sunflower seeds." Ade touched them in wonder. "Before Mary brung me here, I gave them to Bull. Told him to hide them until another Gardener girl showed up."

Eden stared down at the seeds, letting the revelation settle on her skin. Her mother had held these seeds. She had brought them to this spirit world.

"They got ruined when Mother Mary stole my gift. I . . . I think they're dead now."

"Don't nothing die," Ade said. "Only change."

Eden wanted to believe the woman, but the bleached seeds felt useless in her hands. What could she do now? She took a deep breath, inhaling the damp smell of the dirt floor. But then she remembered Bull's words. *You gon' know where to sow them.*

She slowly stood up and moved to the center of the room. "I'm going to plant them here." Her voice was defiant in the darkness.

The elder spirits surrounded her. Ade and Netty dug a shallow hole with their hands, and Eden gently placed the seeds in the dirt and covered them.

Netty knelt beside her and bowed her head. It wasn't a burial or a time for mourning. It was a time for believing in beginnings. A sowing for a new birth.

Eden pressed her hands over the mound, thinking of her mother surrounded by blooms in the summer garden. Sun on her skin. Happiness in her heart.

She pressed her love onto the seeds. The emotion of her true essence, even in death. Intense sorrow and pure joy. Light and dark. Memories of her mother that lay deep in Eden's soul. This was a gift that could never be stolen.

The circle of spirits crept closer, their whispers growing in the gloom. Eden closed her eyes. Underneath her fingers, the mound trembled, growing warm under her touch.

Eden pushed the last shreds of her hope into the seeds. The spirits around her chanted, their frail voices bouncing off the walls. A sharp jolt went up Eden's arm and she snatched her hands away.

The mound quivered and a tiny sprout pushed out from the soil.

CHAPTER THIRTY-NINE

Flowers in the Dark

Eden gasped in wonder as the sprout unfurled along with other fledging buds, breaking through the soil fresh and green.

The spirits widened their circle, their eyes glinting as the seedlings grew into tall stalks, unrolling leaves that wavered in the gloom.

Ade regarded the blossoming plants that surrounded her. "What they say be true. Ain't nothing a Gardener can't grow."

Netty clapped her hands and laughed. Buds split open to reveal yellow petals, bright and luminous like streaks of the sun. They leaned toward Eden, touching her face. The center of each sunflower was like a velvet brown eye. Long threads of pollen floated in the air and settled on Eden's arms. The golden dust disappeared into her skin, and a faint buzz vibrated in her bones.

The dark room brightened as the sunflowers continued to grow, and the elder spirits rejoiced in the burgeoning light.

Strong roots rumbled beneath the soil and finally buckled free. Ophelie held tight to Eden as sunflower leaves and stalks crawled up the walls and filled the crevices. The elder spirits gathered closer together as the plants expanded around the room.

"They looking for a way out," Ade said.

Bursting from the dirt floor, the roots squeezed underneath the door with a low rumble. The elder spirits cowered at the sound, their voices low and fearful. Bright green leaves covered the wooden surface of the door until a loud crack filled the room. The strong roots split the frame in half, and the door plunged to the floor in a cloud of dust.

Eden stood stunned as the sunflowers raced out of the room. Slowly, the elder spirits proceeded to the open doorway, their feet trampling on the cracked wooden slab. More roots burrowed under doors across the hallway, rolling like distant thunder. They breached the remaining doors, and the openings gaped like dark wounds.

Weak and yellowed eyes blinked in the gloom, and more spirits filtered out of their captive spaces. Cries of recognition filled the hallway. They held tight to their kindred spirits. Some had been reunited with family, others with beloved friends. All of them now free from the witch's prison.

Eden was surrounded by the elder spirits and their joyful reunions, but she kept her eyes focused farther down the hallway. An approaching light flickered down the stairs. Eden remained still as a shadowed figure holding a lantern appeared. The elder spirits stopped speaking and held still, waiting to see if the witch had come down to investigate the commotion. Netty grabbed Eden's hand.

But then the figure turned and looked back up the stairs, and the muffled voice of a girl filtered down through the hallway, followed by tumbling footsteps. Ruby, Lorenzo, and Isaac clambered to the bottom of the stairs. Behind them, Bull emerged from the shadows, holding a lantern and a large ax.

Ade rushed down the hallway to her sister, and they collided into a tight embrace. Netty and Eden quickly followed to greet the brothers.

"We knew something had gone wrong when y'all didn't come to meet us," Isaac said.

"Bull finally told Ruby what Mother Mary done," Lorenzo said. "Took a few moons to get him to side with us."

Eden turned to the witch's servant. His face was young, and the copper pennies on his eyelids glinted in the lantern light.

"I couldn't take it no more, Little Eden," he said. "Ain't right what Miss Mary been doing. These children help set my mind to chop down them doors. But seem like you done that for me."

"I sowed the seeds," Eden told him.

"Your Gardener gift is strong," Bull said, marveling at roots traveling along the walls.

"We need to head out," Ruby said. "Moon gon' be rising soon, and Mother Mary bound to return."

They guided the elder spirits up the stairs. Ophelie held tight to Eden's arm, and she helped the old woman carefully up each step. In the great room, the sunflowers, leaves, and roots covered the furniture.

The black snake lay scattered on the floor, cut in several pieces by Bull's ax. The stripe was gone, and its forked tongue lolled from its head, no longer a threat.

Grace and Almond were piled against each other, their hands tied tight with long scraps of white cloth. The older girl's glare was cold and angry as she struggled against her bondage.

"Mother Mary gon' ruin all y'all!" she yelled at them.

"We ain't gon' be here when that leech come back," Ruby spat.

The young girl scowled in hatred as Netty pushed her away from the bound couple. Eden ushered Ophelie to the glass doors, but she turned to look at the painting above the fireplace. The sunflowers had covered most of it, nestling inside the jagged hole. Renata Spelling stood in the doorway of the sitting room, watching them. The former owner of the mansion had a look of glee on her face as she watched the leaves and roots overtake the great room.

Bull emerged from the stairs with the last remaining spirits. He paused, following Eden's stare. "Don't worry about her none."

Eden and Bull guided the rest of the Everdark spirits onto the mansion's portico. Although the eyes of the elders seemed brighter, they were still empty husks. Weak and powerless.

"Where are we going?" Eden asked Ruby.

"To my sister's house," she answered. "Then to Pirate Island."

Eden knew it would be a slow journey getting the elder spirits to the frost-covered house, and she wondered if they could make it before the moonrise. The witch had already proven that the moon didn't dictate her return, and a small panic rose in Eden.

"We need to hurry." She took Ophelie's hand again, and the old woman smiled at her with gratitude. "You ready to leave?"

"Been ready," the old woman answered.

Eden turned her gaze to the greenhouse. The glass building

had been shattered, a jagged skeleton in the night. Roses with long, curved thorns crawled along the exposed beams. Other flowers rose high into star-filled sky. Thick roots roamed along the grand lawn, making the ground tremble. The strong fragrance of flowers mixed with the salt air.

More sunflowers charged onto the portico, covering the wide columns and intertwining with the other roots and plants from the greenhouse. The spirits watched in awe as the roots bonded and braided together into one gigantic stem, and then stormed like a tornado across the grand lawn to the courtyard behind the mansion.

Ade and Ruby collected the group of spirits, preparing for the trek through the orange grove and into the woods. The elders seemed stronger now that they had been freed from their prison, and hope swelled in Eden's chest. They would get these spirits away from the mansion and then figure out what came next.

But then a vengeful cry cut through the night, sharp and angry. Eden's hope shriveled and was replaced with an icy dread.

The Witch of Everdark surged out of the woods, her face twisted with rage.

CHAPTER FORTY
The Witch's Wrath

The witch was wearing her night-walking clothes. Loose hair shrouded her face in a dark halo, and a thousand tiny stars shimmered on her indigo skin. Her eyes were solid black and filled with hatred. As she stalked across the grand lawn, palmetto trees snapped and collapsed to the ground, fueled by her rage.

Sunflowers and roots shrank from her presence, withering under the starlight. Eden shuddered in fear. The Witch of Everdark still ruled this world with her vengeful magic.

"Mother Mary!" Grace screamed from the mansion's open doors. The older girl had broken free, torn strips of cloth dangling from her wrists. Almond appeared next to her and calmly blinked, oblivious of the pending doom.

The witch marched toward the mansion, but the spirits remained locked in place. When Eden struggled to move, she only could manage a few steps with arduous labor. They were pinned under the witch's magic, trapped and powerless.

"Maybe she take mercy on us," Ophelie said, her voice weak and scared.

The witch rose into the air, and wisps of black smoke curled from her long, sharp nails, enveloping her in a ghastly aura.

"The audacity to dishonor me," the witch bellowed. "To disrespect my land *and* my house!"

Eden's body remained locked by the witch's power. Ruby shouted in frustration, while Ade struggled hopelessly against the forcible hold. After several tries, the woman huffed in defeat and narrowed her eyes at the witch.

"Miss Mary, you need to leave us be," Bull said, straining against the witch's magical chains.

The witch hovered above them as a strong wind blew her long hair away from her face. Mary Turner was horrid and beautiful at once, her magic flaring in waves of hatred. She raised her arms and a sharp clap of lighting struck the ground, releasing the spirits from their trapped positions. But then the elder spirits wailed, scratching at their necks.

"Stop it!" Eden cried.

"I hid them away from Old Buzzard," the witch said. "They was protected by my grace!"

"You kept them as prisoners!" Ruby screamed.

"Old Buzzard only come here after you stole from us," Ade said, locking eyes with the witch. "And them Turner women ain't never gon' answer your call. Ain't no ancestor coming for you."

"Shut your mouth about my sisters!" The witch's hands clenched into tight fists as the wind whipped harder. Beneath her, roots curled and blackened while sunflowers withered and died. They were no match against the witch's magic.

The elder spirits fell to the ground, gasping for air. Ophelie dropped to her knees, bowing her head in sorrow. When Eden reached down to help her, the old woman stopped her.

"Leave me be," she said between gasps. "Done . . . fighting."

The buzz that Eden had felt in her bones below the mansion had faded. The sunflowers, once strong enough to rip doors off hinges, now lay around her dying. The witch was winning.

Grace darted across the grand lawn to stand below the hovering witch. Almond remained on the mansion's portico, his face revealing no emotion.

"Mother Mary, they tied me up!" the older girl cried. "They cut open your snake!"

The witch gazed down at her oldest daughter. "They gon' pay for disrespecting you."

Roots dissolved into ash and blew away in the wind, the film covering Eden's tongue. It was the true taste of Everdark, where everything underneath was rot. The witch was using her magic to wield pain and torture, the anger making her ruthless. The spirits choked and wailed. Sounds of anguish filled the air.

Bull lay on his side, his cream cardigan now streaked with the ash of dead roots, his face no longer smooth and young. Lorenzo held Isaac to his chest as the little boy convulsed. Ade and Ruby stood their ground, but they both grasped at their necks as they struggled to breathe. The witch continued to thrust her power upon them, showing no mercy.

Eden closed her eyes to the turmoil. The witch's cruelty hadn't affected her like the others. The low buzz in her bones had returned, thrumming like a heartbeat in her ears.

The sunflowers she'd planted in the dark had given their last wisp of power to her. Her Gardener gift was weak, but it would have to be enough.

She opened her eyes. The witch still hovered above them in a ghoulish shadow. Eden sank to the ground, touching blades of burned grass and digging her fingers into the soil. Warmth traveled up her arms, and green shards of light burrowed into the ground. The soil trembled beneath her fingers, illuminating as the last of her Gardener gift traveled underground. Across the lawn, dead roots and sunflowers shuddered back to life.

The witch hovered closer to Eden. "Your little gift ain't gon' save you. I done took the best of it."

Eden lifted her head. The witch thought she was stronger, but Eden remembered the essence of what had brought the fallow seeds to life below the mansion. The memories, the love, and even the sadness. It was what had connected her to the Gardener lineage. The mothers and daughters. The ones who had healed and reclaimed the soil. The women who survived bondage and terror. The women who shared their land with others after freedom. Their blood ran through Eden's veins.

The buzz in her bones grew stronger, and she quivered with its force. Roots re-formed from ash and coiled around her waist, covering her arms and legs. Fresh leaves sprouted over her skin. They gleamed with green light, pulsing like the heartbeat of a bright girl and growing stronger.

The witch grimaced and lashed out with sharp darts of magic toward her. But the leaves had left no part of her skin exposed and protected Eden from the witch's attack.

Ade gagged, struggling to move to Eden's side. The woman's breathing was labored and weak. Her voice was a faint whisper in the wind.

"Call upon your family now. Let them hear you. *Let them come.*"

Eden inhaled sharply as the roots tightened and dug into her skin. They sank deep into her bones. Her mother had come to Everdark with seeds. She had drawn sketches of the spirits from their shared dreams. Eden felt the presence of her mother, her grandmother, all the Gardener women she had never met, whose names she would never know. The ones who came across the water to Safina Island. The ones who had stayed and the ones who had flown away.

"Hear me, please," Eden whispered weakly into the shrieking wind among the suffering and turmoil of the other spirits. "Mom. Granny Alma. Everyone. Help me free this world."

CHAPTER FORTY-ONE

A Mother's Choice

The roots twitched on Eden's body. The witch still floated above them. Beautiful and powerful. Eden stared up at her, eyes blurry with tears.

Beneath her, the soil softly rumbled like a low growl, and the witch hesitated in her torture. Then the wind stopped and a thick silence filled the night. Clouds cleared the sky and bright starlight covered the spirits.

A loud whoosh echoed from the courtyard, like an incoming train, and the large, braided stem returned, careening onto the grand lawn. In a tornado of movement, it rushed toward the witch, and she lunged an attack with her long, sharp nails, but the stem dodged away from the threat.

The opponents circled each other in a menacing dance. The witch grabbed the braided stem and screamed, a feral sound erupting in the air. The intertwined roots bulged in her grasp, and then a cavernous mouth opened. A chorus of women's voices fill the air, the Gardeners answering Eden's call. The braided stem's mouth expanded wider and bent down to swallow the witch whole.

Sunflowers shattered through the mansion's windows, and Grace screamed and fell to the ground, covering her head. Roots erupted from the foundation, and the tabby walls cracked. Now that the witch's magic had been stunted, the elder spirits around Eden regained their breath. They huddled together as the mansion was overtaken by roots and leaves.

The braided stem still hovered in the air, but now it jerked haphazardly and finally fell to the ground in a thundering thud. It thrashed wildly until it split open.

The witch rose from its carcass, covered in slime. She shrieked in anger and red sparks of magic singed the split stem until it burned. The fire's glow illuminated the witch in a vengeful silhouette. She stumbled toward the spirits, her black eyes filled with rage. But she was now weak. When she lashed out with her nails, only a trickle of smoke curled into the air.

The greenhouse roses sped across the grand lawn. They gathered in whirling funnels and crashed upon the witch. She screamed in shock and frustration. More greenhouse plants and flowers came to throttle her, devouring the witch like a bounty, covering her with their weight until she crumpled to the ground. Blackness drained from the witch's eyes, and they glowed a sickly yellow while her indigo skin drained away.

Thorns trapped her in a tight prison. They covered the witch's now dark brown skin, and she gagged as the thorns entered her mouth. She twisted and screamed, pleading for her sisters to save her. But no aid arrived from the Turner women. The witch whimpered for mercy while the thorns enveloped her.

"I'm so tired," the witch finally cried. "Tired of everything."

Dark clouds blotted out the starlight, and Eden watched the night sky with frightful anticipation. Her fears heightened when

Old Buzzard appeared, circling low around them. The elder spirits ducked and scattered to hide, but Eden's terror kept her from moving.

The god-spirit landed on the grand lawn, his claws scraping against the roots. The plants and flowers cowered away from the god-spirit. He approached the witch and pecked at the thorns. They quickly dissolved to ash, freeing the witch from her prison. Stepping away, he waited for the witch to stand.

But Mary Turner remained on her knees, her sobs filling the night with her despair. She had lost her stolen power, and now she had a choice to make. Old Buzzard tilted his blood-red head and waited patiently for the witch's answer.

She slowly rose to face the god-spirit, but then she met Eden's eyes. Tears flowed down the witch's cheeks, sadness etched on her face. The world she had made was ruined.

Eden knew the witch's life had been stolen. Her talent had been wasted, her dreams had been extinguished. The world had never given her what she'd truly deserved. Everdark had been her chance to live the life she had always wanted. Now, in the end, it still hadn't been enough.

The witch's tears had now stopped, and even in defeat, she remained stunningly beautiful. Netty emerged from the shadows and stood beside Eden. The witch's daughters waited for their fates.

Mary Turner fixed her gaze on Old Buzzard. After a few moments, she huffed out a small chuckle and lifted her chin.

"Only took what I deserved. I should let you take this world. But I can't let you take my daughters."

Old Buzzard spread out his wings and let out an angry caw, but the witch was no longer afraid of the god-spirit. She moved toward him, defiant and brave.

"The answer still no."

Above them, the dark clouds churned away. An ethereal light as bright as the moon shone down over them, and the god-spirit stumbled back, as if harmed by its glow. Mary Turner tilted her head up to the silver light and smiled.

"Told you my sisters was coming," the witch said.

The elder spirits emerged from their hiding places. They watched as the witch raised her arms in surrender. Mary Turner rose in the night sky, her clothes and hair wavering around her in the air.

She hovered above the spirits, but this time there was no fear of the witch's wrath. She looked down at Eden and Netty, her face now serene and peaceful.

"Goodbye, daughters," she said, her voice full of regret but also a mother's love.

Her body ascended into the sky, burning bright. The clouds pulsed and reflected in pale colors until Mary Turner dissolved into a silver mist.

Old Buzzard bellowed out another angry caw, but there was nothing he could do to take this world now. He turned to the other spirits, hulking over each of them. But none of them took his offer.

When he came to Eden, she dropped to her knees, whimpering as he placed his heavy claw on her head. Filtered images engulfed her mind. Her father smiling at the breakfast table.

Her mother laughing in the summer garden. The three of them together again. A life where her mother had never died and grief didn't exist. The roots churned inside Eden with longing.

This was Old Buzzard's offer for her, but Eden knew none of it was real. Like Everdark, it was a dark magic that wouldn't last. If she took this offer, she would be bound to the god-spirit forever. It was a price she wasn't willing to pay.

"No," she whispered.

Old Buzzard lifted his heavy claw from Eden's head. He took off into the air, ripping open a jagged scar to another world filled with red and purple clouds. When the god-spirit darted through, the sky healed and revealed bright stars.

A loud rumble drew Eden's attention to the mansion. More fractures appeared in the tabby walls, leaving gaping holes until they crumbled in plumes of dust. The spirits retreated as the mansion built with the witch's stolen magic finally fell.

Grace's screams filled the void as she hovered over a body of ash. It was Almond, the boy she loved. The conjured spirit had met the same demise as the mansion.

The older girl stood up, her green-striped day dress soiled with her true love's ashes. She gazed empty-eyed at Eden but didn't speak. Grace turned away from the spirits and drifted into the orange grove, disappearing into the shadows of the trees.

"Nothing we can do for her now," Netty whispered. "Leave her be. What's done been done."

Eden stood in astonishment with the other spirits. Everything the witch had conjured in this world had been destroyed. The leaves covering her body fluttered and small white blooms pushed through Eden's skin. The flowers floated down to the ash-covered ground, and the voices of the Gardener and Turner women echoed in the air.

"Thank you, thank you, thank you," they whispered.

The seashell path to the ocean lay beyond the ruins of the mansion. The night sky was fading, and a glint of light edged the horizon.

The sun was finally rising.

CHAPTER FORTY-TWO

The Sunrise Beach

The spirits passed through a veil of ash. Netty and Eden walked in their tattered dresses and dusty boots. Tendrils of orange-tinged clouds drifted above them.

The black sand beach had been transformed. Shifting colors of pink and white grains shimmered under the lightening sky. Eden grabbed a handful of sand, letting it fall through her fingers.

Waves crashed against the shore as the spirits spread out on the beach. The sun rose over the ocean's horizon, a bright orb of radiant yellow. The elder spirits praise danced, clapping their hands and stomping their feet.

Eden's dark brown skin had returned, while Netty's tone gleamed a warm amber. A kaleidoscope of shades celebrated happily on the beach. The bound spirits were now free.

The little girl took Eden's hand and danced with the elders, following them in the counterclockwise circle of the ring shout, singing the songs of their ancestors. Bull moved along with them, his face young and full of joy. The pennies were now gone, and his warm brown eyes twinkled in the sunlight. Ade and Ruby clapped their hands and sang proudly while Lorenzo and Isaac swayed their bodies to the rhythm and voices.

After the celebration and fellowship, some of the elder spirits gathered with their reunited family and departed to the places they had dwelled in the spirit world before the witch's reign.

The remaining spirits lingered on the beach, staring at the sun with tears streaming down their cheeks. Ophelie approached Eden, her gait now strong and sure. When she smiled, her kind eyes crinkled in gratitude.

"You done good," the old woman said. "Been waiting for dayclean to come."

Eden remembered Uncle Willie's definition of the word. *A fresh day. When light banish the dark.*

"What will you do now?" she asked.

Ophelie watched the other spirits traveling down the beach toward the woods. "I reckon some folks would stay now this world done got back right. Get unfinished business in order. But my people calling me. I can hear them now."

Lorenzo and Isaac approached them, their deep-brown skin glowing in the sunshine.

"Time for us to move on, Eden," the older boy said.

A lump formed in her throat. The brothers had helped her when she'd washed up on Pirate Island's shore. She would be forever grateful. Eden gave Isaac a tight hug. "Take care of your brother."

The little boy wrapped his arms around her waist. "You gon' see your people soon."

The older boy nodded in agreement, but then his face turned somber. "I hate it turn out this way for you, but you freed us and now you free."

"You can walk with us," Ophelie offered.

Eden searched for Netty on the beach. She spotted the little girl with Bull. They were sitting in the sand with Ade and Ruby, watching the waves. Eden wasn't quite ready to leave yet.

"No, you go on," she told them. "I have unfinished business myself."

Ophelie kissed Eden on the cheek. "Bless you, child."

The brothers took the old woman's hand. They walked together to the ocean, their bare feet dusted with bright pink sand. They waded into the waves, but soon they floated into the air, their bodies light and free. Isaac's laugh drifted in the wind, bright like the sun. The spirits floated higher into the blue sky, among the clouds, until they faded into a golden mist.

Eden blinked away tears as she joined the last of the remaining spirits on the beach. Netty ran to her in childlike joy. She was the spirit who had become her chosen sister. She had held Eden's hand on her first night in Everdark, and Netty's would be the last hand Eden held before moving on.

"Thank you for everything," Eden said.

"No need for thanking me," the little girl said. "You saved us."

Eden smiled at Netty, but she knew that she wasn't the only one who had saved them. Mary Turner had saved them too. In the end, she had chosen her daughters.

The little girl took her hand and they walked to join the other spirits. Bull rested in the sand, his eyes focused on the ocean's horizon, deep in thought. Ade and Ruby were pressed close together, finally reunited.

"We gon' head out to my house," Ade said.

"You can come with us," Ruby offered. "More than welcome."

Eden hesitated. Although Everdark had been destroyed, she knew this spirit world wasn't where she truly belonged.

Netty squeezed Eden's hand. "She ain't coming with us."

Bull stood up, brushing the sand from his clothes, his posture strong and distinguished. "Walk well, Little Eden."

More tears sprang to Eden's eyes as the spirit embraced her. "Thank you."

Ade watched them with a gentle smile on her face. "If you change your mind, you know where to find us."

She hugged the sisters, giving Ruby an understanding nod. She had forgiven the spirit for her betrayal. Ruby had wanted to save Ade, and Eden now knew that she would have done the same for Netty.

The little girl wrapped her in one last embrace, tears wet on her face. "Walk well, bright girl," she whispered into Eden's ear.

After the farewells, the spirits trekked up the dunes to the seashell path. The land was already healing and returning to its origins, a true mirror of Safina Island.

Now alone on the beach, Eden sat down and took off her boots. She pressed her toes into the bright pink sand, staring at the shimmering grains on her brown skin. The sun was above her, and the ocean waves were tranquil and beautiful. She was in a spiritual paradise. A place where her ancestors had traveled for respite after their heavy burdens of the living world.

Eden had plenty of unfinished business, but none of it could be sorted out here. She couldn't say goodbye to her father or give Natalie one last hug. Those things had been taken from her.

She knew that staying in this spirit world wouldn't help her cope with these regrets.

It was time to let go and move on, but a blossoming fear spread on her skin. Eden hadn't come to terms with her own death and what it meant. What would happen next? How would she find her mother? Granny Alma? Her Gardener ancestors? What if she got lost?

Eden stood up, pressing her toes into the sand. She focused on the waves cresting the shore. It was time for her to walk and rise. But then behind her, she heard a voice.

"Eden, I've missed you."

CHAPTER FORTY-THREE
Beloved Nora

Eden's mother was wearing a T-shirt and jeans. Dirt smudged her cheek and collarbone. She looked the same as she had that day in the summer garden.

Eden rushed into her mother's arms, and the memories unleashed from her bones. "I've missed you so much, Mom," she cried. "I've been so sad. Then I came here and I couldn't get back. I thought I would be lost forever."

"It's all right now," her mother said, wiping tears from Eden's face.

"Did you come to get me?" she asked. "I didn't know if I would be able to find you, but I'm ready to go."

Her mother's smile dimmed. "What you've done for this world, breaking it free from the dark, I'm in awe. It's why I can come here and see you now."

Eden took a trembling breath. "I planted the seeds. The ones you brought here."

"Yes, you did, my love." Her mother's smile returned, wide and proud. "You did what I wasn't able to do. So when you called to us, we answered."

"Where are we going next? I'm so scared."

Her mother placed her hands on both sides of Eden's face,

looking deep into her eyes. "Never be scared, Eden. There's nothing to fear."

Eden crumbled into another sob. "I didn't get a chance to tell Dad goodbye. Or Natalie. None of the relatives I met in Willow Hammock. They . . . they won't know what happened to me."

"Oh, my love, don't worry about this." Her mother's calm voice soothed her. "You won't have to say goodbye."

Eden took another shaking breath. "I . . . I don't understand. I'm not going with you?"

"I came to see you because I've missed you. So very much," her mother stated. "But it's not your time."

"But . . . but I died."

"Nothing ever dies," her mother said. "It just changes. Your father needs you, as well as other people you have yet to meet. You have so much to do. You need to grow up. Bring your own children into the world. That's why you can't come with me now. It isn't your time. I only came here to tell you how proud I am and that I love you. Always."

Her mother brought Eden close, kissing her forehead. They stood together under the sun and listened to the waves crash against the shore, but then her mother released her embrace.

"You'll walk well, but not yet," she said.

Eden nodded, unable to speak. Her mother removed stray curls from her face. Then she turned and walked toward the ocean waves. Rising into the air, Eden's mother disappeared in a golden burst of mist.

Eden sank to her knees and wept. Her mother was gone

again. She curled into a ball on the pink sand, the grains scratching her wet face.

After Eden emptied her tears, she rolled onto her back. The sun had crested behind the dunes and the sky was solid blue. She remained a spirit with a heart that still lay dormant in her chest. No blood rushed through her veins. But there was no burden pressing down on her. No hollow feelings of regret. She would always miss her mother, but the block of ice had finally melted.

In the distance, a dark shape approached. As it ventured closer, Eden realized it was the black cat.

She bolted up from the sand as the black cat crept closer. She stopped a few feet in front of Eden, her goldenrod eyes staring with a type of knowing. A loud purr rumbled from her body, and her fluffy tail whipped at the pink sand.

"The cat that moves between worlds," Eden whispered.

The black cat stepped closer and released a gentle meow. Eden's mother had said that it wasn't her time yet. She was meant to return to the world of the living. Now Eden understood that the black cat had come to take her back.

Reaching out with a trembling hand, she stroked the cat's thick fur, which was lush and soft. Another strong purr vibrated from the black cat, and a scratchy tongue licked Eden's skin.

A warmth entered her body. White-hot heat that didn't burn, but rose like a fever, forming beads of sweat on her forehead. Dizziness overtook her and she stumbled, the pink sand pillowing her fall. Eden shivered and panted. Her vision glazed over with multicolored stars. Then the fever broke and the heat left her body. The black cat was still there, eyes luminous in the sunlight. Eden stretched out on the sand, folding her hands over her chest.

A strong heartbeat pulsed under her fingers.

Eden gasped as the spirit world whirled away. The thumping of her heart bounced in her ears. She whirred with incredible speed through a brilliant tunnel. Voices zipped past her and a loud, humming buzz surrounded her, until there was silence.

She was in a large field, and the sun was above her in an intense blue sky. Her ears popped in a whoosh, and then she heard voices calling her name.

Sitting up in the tall grass, Eden winced at the pain in her head, an aching throb at the base of her skull. The day dress with mother-of-pearl buttons was clean and fresh, but her bare feet still shimmered with pink sand.

The tall grass shielded her from viewing the surroundings, but Eden knew that she was somewhere on Big Savannah. The large meadow on Safina Island. She was back in the world of the living.

Eden heard the voices again. Partially hidden as she was in the tall grass, no one would see her. She would have to answer their call.

"I'm here," she replied in a weak whisper.

The voices were closer now, but Eden knew that they hadn't heard her. "I'm here! I'm here!"

A tumble of steps approached, figures cutting through the tall grass. They found her with grasping hands and questions.

"Eden!" Her father's voice was hoarse and dry. "We've been

looking for you all over. I thought . . ." He broke down, his cries echoing through the meadow. Dr. Leopold buried his face in his daughter's neck. "I couldn't lose you, too."

Uncle Willie rushed beside them. "You gave us a mighty fright, Little Eden. What made you decide to go out walking without telling nobody?"

Gardener relatives and other island folks from Willow Hammock surrounded her. They all gazed upon her like she was a priceless jewel.

"I'm sorry," Eden finally said. "I got lost and then I guess . . . I fell asleep."

"Don't worry about that now," Uncle Willie said. "Only been a few hours since we started looking for you."

When Eden had left to venture into the woods behind Aunt Susanna's house, it had been early morning, and now the sun was high in the afternoon sky. But Eden knew she had dwelled much longer in Everdark.

"Are you hurt?" her father asked.

Eden shook her head as Dr. Leopold and her great-uncle helped her to her feet. She tried her best not to wobble. They led her to the main road and waited as one of her cousins fetched Uncle Willie's truck. Eden sat snug against her father, safe and loved as they drove back to Aunt Susanna's mint-green house.

Dr. Leopold pulled her close, kissing her forehead. "I'm never letting you out of my sight again," he whispered.

"I've missed you, Dad," Eden replied. "I'm glad you found me."

CHAPTER FORTY-FOUR
A New Life

When they had returned from Big Savannah, the yard had been filled with neighbors and relatives. Little Betsy and Miss Melba touched Eden's face, tutting concerns, and their husbands regarded her with care. Miss Nadine nodded at her knowingly with her blue-rimmed eyes.

Aunt Susanna had ushered her into the house and loaded a plate with fresh drop biscuits and savory red peas. After being satisfied that she had eaten enough, her great-aunt let Eden bathe and then covered her with a quilt.

Now as Eden stirred from her sleep, Aunt Susanna straightened, wiping her eyes. "You rest well?" she asked.

Eden nodded. She was in her pajamas, so different from the Everdark nightgown trimmed with lace.

"I was so worried about you, Little Eden," her great-aunt said.

"I'm sorry," she responded.

Aunt Susanna patted Eden's leg, but then her face turned serious, as if remembering a haunted memory, and Eden's heart sped up. "You was wearing something different when you returned to the house. Ain't seen a day dress like that since I was a kid. And even then, it was only in pictures."

Eden swallowed. None of the others had said anything, but she had seen the look on Miss Nadine's face. The certainty that she had been elsewhere. The old woman had known that Eden had crossed over into the spirit world and returned.

"I was in Everdark," Eden whispered. "It was a bad place . . . but not anymore."

Aunt Susanna took a long sigh. "I didn't wanna believe none of this. But after seeing you in them clothes, the truth was plain to see. Your mama told us that's where she had been, but I thought she was delirious. Your granny wasn't no better. Told me Nora was the last Gardener girl who could cross over. But I dismissed it all as a bunch of mess."

"It's all true," Eden confirmed.

Her great-aunt looked into her eyes. "I ain't never had no shine, so I never understood it. It had been so long since a Gardener girl was born full of magic. Until your mama. But even then, I didn't believe it. Then your granny and your mama went to the mainland, and seem like they stop believing too."

But Eden knew they hadn't forgotten. Granny Alma had shared the island stories. It was why her mother hadn't destroyed the sketchbook. She had crossed into Everdark to save her ancestors, bringing seeds cultivated with Gardener blood. But the plat-eye had almost consumed her. Nora Gardener had failed in her mission, and it was a memory that had haunted her.

"The black cat brought me back," Eden said. "The same one I saw at the Renata Mansion. Does she have a name?"

Aunt Susanna arranged the quilt around Eden, enveloping her in warmth and love. "Folks say she ain't got no name because she older than Safina. The highest of god-spirits. If she brought you back, it was for a good reason. She gave you a new life."

When her great-aunt left, Eden stayed in bed and slept until nightfall. When she woke up, she went to the window and opened the curtains to the darkness. In the night sky, the moon covered everything in silver light. Eden remembered the north-wing bedroom in the witch's mansion. The courtyard and the seashell path that led to the ocean. Netty, with her loving hugs. Grace, with her eternal frown. She hoped that the older girl had found a way to move on. By now, Lorenzo and Isaac had been reunited with their father. Ophelie would be with her family too.

Maybe now in the spirit world, Bull was sitting in front of Ade's wood-burning stove, warmed by the fire. He would have a book in his lap, reciting the words he had once longed to learn. Ruby would be there too, listening as she sipped nettle tea with her sister. Now the elders in Willow Hammock could transition after death into this world and greet these spirits for fellowship.

The next morning, Eden sat at the kitchen, where her father sipped coffee. He gave her a smile and motioned for her to give him a hug. She launched herself into his arms, happy to be safe in his embrace.

Uncle Willie opened the screen door, his musical voice filtering to them. "Time to head back to the mainland."

Relatives and neighbors waited in the yard to say their goodbyes and give presents. Miss Nadine came forth with a small bag of seeds.

"Take these back with you," the elder said.

Eden gently held the bag in her hands. "What kind of seeds are these?"

Miss Nadine grinned. "You gon' need to sow them and see."

Little Betsy and Miss Melba gave Eden long, tight hugs while their husbands patiently waited their turn. She laughed and shed happy tears. Eden had found the connection to her mother's lineage. She knew that she wasn't leaving the island completely, because Safina was in her blood.

Aunt Susanna ushered them to Uncle Willie's truck, a wet towel on her shoulder. "Don't be a stranger now. I don't wanna have to wait another whole year to see y'all again."

"We'll come again soon," Dr. Leopold said. "We promise."

Uncle Willie drove them down the dirt road, and Eden leaned out the window, smelling the salty air. The sun was bright, and she closed her eyes and let the island wind soothe her skin.

At the dock, they retrieved their suitcases from the truck and boarded the *Safina Queen*. Her great-uncle revved the engine as Eden sat starboard with her father. The island loomed behind them, lush and green.

"Water kind of choppy in the sound today," her great-uncle said over the engine. "Y'all make sure to stay settled in."

As they departed, a small figure emerged from the stout palmettos. The black cat wandered onto the dock. She sat at the edge and watched them leave, flicking her tail.

Dr. Leopold took Eden's hand and brought it to his lips for a soft kiss, and she turned to look her father in the eyes. Her mother had been right. Eden needed to return to the world of the living. Her father still needed her as much as she needed him.

"Thank you for bringing me to the island," Eden said.

"It wasn't too much, was it?" he asked.

"No," Eden answered truthfully. "It wasn't too much."

When she peered back at the dock, the island of her ances-tors was smaller in the distance, and the black cat was gone.

CHAPTER FORTY-FIVE

A Summer Garden

E den and her father had started their road trip back to
Maryland, but now they were at a rest stop in North
Carolina. Eden sat at a picnic table with the map spread
out before her. She stared at the Georgia sea islands on the blue
expanse of the Atlantic Ocean. Her finger circled over Safina
Island, her mother's birthplace.

When her phone buzzed, she opened her macramé bag to
answer the call.

"Are you back yet?" Natalie asked.

"We're still on the road," Eden answered. "About halfway."

"How was your trip? How many relatives did you meet? Did
you go to the beach? Why do you sound different?"

Eden smiled at her best friend's rash of questions. She wondered if, when she returned to Maryland, Natalie would be able to
see the roots underneath her skin, the glimmer of shine, the power
of her Gardener gift. Eden had crossed over into a spirit world of
eternal night, defeated a witch, and freed kindred spirits.

"I'm kind of different now," she answered. "I learned a lot
about my family and the island."

When she was ready, Eden would share what had happened
with her. She would tell her best friend everything. But for now,

she wanted to keep it inside her like the roots wrapped around her beating heart.

"I hope going there didn't make you too sad," Natalie said, her voice softer.

"I was sad at first. Very sad," Eden admitted, thinking of her time in Everdark when everything seemed hopeless and eternal. "But on the island, I realized Mom will always be with me."

Eden now knew that the spirit world was a mirror, and she was closer to her ancestors than she could have ever imagined.

She said goodbye to Natalie and waited for her father to return from the rest stop vending machines. She grinned as Dr. Leopold approached with sodas and several bags of chips.

"When we get back home, no more junk food or sodas," her father said. "Only water and balanced meals."

"Deal," Eden laughed.

Dr. Leopold sat at the picnic table across from her, the map between them and the sun high in the sky. At that moment, Eden felt a jolt of happiness. A hope for the future and what it could hold. She knew her grief would reappear again, and she would still feel the deep sorrow of losing her mother. But she also knew there was nothing to fear. Nothing ever truly died, it only changed. Her mother lived in her memories. She would embrace the sadness along with the joy.

Eden thought of the seeds that Miss Nadine had given her and what would sprout from them. They could be herbs or flowers. She wouldn't know until she sowed them deep into the soil. It didn't matter what grew from them, because the seeds were from the heart of Safina Island.

The black cat had brought her back to the world of the living. Eden had things to do and people to meet. In the world of the dead, she knew what the power of memories and the love of family could do. They could conquer many things, chase away darkness and bring forth light. Safina was in her blood, and the Gardener gift lay deep in her bones. This power would be with her. Always.

"I've made a decision," Eden told her father. "I'm going to start a summer garden. Do you want to help me plant some seeds?"

ACKNOWLEDGMENTS

I wrote this novel in 2020 during the height of a global pandemic. It was a story I needed to tell just for me, and I feel extremely blessed to share it with others.

I want to give thanks to my agent, Patrice Caldwell, who saw the potential in this novel and became its champion.

For my editor, Kendra Levin, who had the belief that I could shape Eden's story into something beautifully dark and magical.

To the Simon & Schuster BFYR team who helped bring this book into the world. Special thanks to Jenica Nasworthy and Amanda Ramirez.

To art director Sarah Creech and artist Kaitlin June Edwards for the gorgeous cover and Hilary Zarycky for the interior design.

To copy editor Megan Gendell and proofreader Ariel So for their expertise and respect for the novel's colloquialisms and dialect.

For Samira Ahmed, Hanna Alkaf, Kelly Barnhill, Hayley Chewins, Dhonielle Clayton, Heather Kassner, Kwame Mbalia, and Anne Ursu, who offered such wonderful words about this book. I admire the work of these authors, so their praise is truly an honor.

For Nafiza Azad, Natalie Kaes, and Lisa Moore Ramée, who read early versions of this novel and provided priceless feedback.

To my friends, family, and dear loved ones who have weathered the storms of these turbulent years. The sun is finally rising.

Most of all, for the readers who have been deeply touched by grief. I hope this novel has given you enough light to bloom.